USA Today Bestselling Author

J.L. BECK
C. HALLMAN

PROLOGUE

Kennedy

What happened? Pain consumes my entire body, my limbs are hard to move, and all I want to do is close my eyes and drift away. My heavy eyelids close with ease.

Wake up. A voice calls, echoing loudly through my mind. Sucking air into my lungs, I gasp at the pungent smell of gasoline that fills my nostrils. My mind is hazy, my thoughts swirling, and nothing makes sense.

Twisting, I realize I can't move. The seat belt digging into my flesh painfully, holding me in place. Though my gaze is blurry, I can make out the form of my best friend. Her slender body sprawled through the shattered windshield, partially lying on the hood of the car. *No!* Her face is covered in blood, coming from large gashes on her forehead.

Bile rises in my throat, making me gag.

"Jillian..." I call out. My voice so raspy, I barely recognize it as my own.

She doesn't move. Her shirt is soaked in red, and my entire body starts to shake. "Jillian, wake up!" Using every ounce of strength I have,

I reach for her. Stretching my body painfully, trying to get to her, but my fingers wrap around nothing but air.

Sirens sound off in the distance, someone is coming to save us. Jillian is going to be okay, she has to be. Staring at her lifeless body, I feel something warm dripping down my face.

Blood. Lifting a hand, I touch the side of my face, running my fingers along the deep gash on my cheek. I'm bleeding, but I don't care. I'm not even scared for myself, but I am terrified for Jillian.

"Jillian! Wake up. Please, wake up. Help is coming," I beg, my lips trembling, and my words slurring. Tears slip down my face as I wait for help to get here.

The closer the sirens get, the further I feel myself slipping away again. It's like my entire body is being wrapped in a blanket. Suddenly, the pain in my limbs drifts away until my whole body goes numb. I can't feel anything, can't make sense of the noises surrounding me. I can't see anything besides my best friend. Her lifeless eyes staring back at me, and her beautiful face ashen.

I think footsteps approach, lights, and sirens blur through the quiet night. But all I can do is stare. Watch. Wishing that it was me...

That I was the one dead.

1

JACKSON

Three days have passed since I found out Kennedy was here at Blackthorn. The blood in my veins turns to ice at the mere thought of her. Her presence is a constant reminder of the night I lost my sister and how much my family has suffered.

Why is she here?

I clench my fist around air, envisioning her throat being in my grasp. The hate I feel for her is all-consuming. It should terrify me. The things I've thought of doing to her should rattle me to the bones, but it doesn't.

Staring at the entrance to the bookstore, I try to act as if I'm not looking for someone. It took me hours to calm myself enough to get to this point. I don't know what the hell I'm doing. All I know is revenge, anger, and hate are burning through me, threatening to take over any rational thinking.

Grinding my teeth hard enough to crack them, I watch as she walks out of the school bookstore. It's like seeing a ghost, but when I blink, she is still there. I'd seen her walking across campus, smiling, happy, *alive*. That was much more than my sister had. She was in the cold, dark ground. No future, no smile. She was part of the earth, and now it's time for Kennedy to pay. She got a slap on her wrist for what happened that night, but I would make sure that she got a real punishment.

My pulse spikes, excitement coating my insides. Now's the time to pounce. As soon as she turns the corner and starts down the alleyway between the two buildings, I move. My feet make little sound as I rush toward her.

She should be smarter, pay closer attention to her surroundings. Then again, she probably wasn't expecting me. I wonder briefly if she knew I was here. If I was part of her choice in coming here.

The first thing to hit me as I get closer to her is her scent. It wafts into my nose, filling my head with memories of a girl I used to love, used to crave. My lip curls in disgust, and I want to punch myself in the cock for thinking about her that way. But such an emotion is impossible to turn off. Even after all this time, she still smells the same, like jasmine and vanilla.

Forget it. Forget her.

Pushing everything but the hate down, I drown myself in the anger and reach for her. My fingers digging into her shoulder. The pads of my fingers burn where I touch her. A gasp escapes her lips as I force her to turn to face me. When I push her back against the brick wall, I become mesmerized, watching as the air expels from her chest.

She's nothing but a bug, a useless tiny bug, and I'm going to squish her.

"Either you're incredibly stupid, or you have a death wish... tell me, which one is it?" I cock my head to the side, examining her shocked features.

Her pink lips part and her hazel eyes widen with confusion, then recognition, and finally fear. It's been years since I saw her last, but as far as I can tell, she looks the same, everything but her hair that is. Her heart-shaped face is framed by long blonde hair. It's a far cry from the chocolate brown she used to be, but I like it better. It makes it easier for me to see her as the killer and less like the girl I used to love. Then it hits me. *Is she trying to hide?*

My gaze drifts from her lips and over to the scar that mars the right side of her face, the skin is raised and a soft pink, that's faded tremendously over time. With a bit of makeup, it's barely noticeable, but I know it's there. I will never forget.

Even with the scar, her beauty is indescribable. She still looks like a goddamn angel sent from heaven. Which I hate more than anything. The thought ignites my anger for her further, and like a match meeting gasoline, I explode. I don't even think as my hand wraps around her delicate throat.

Her pulse thunders under my grip, but she doesn't make an effort to fight me off or run away. I make note of how strange that is but push the thought away before it can latch onto my subconscious. Focusing all my attention on her, I visualize how easy it would be to give her the same fate my sister had been given. Burning rage simmers just beneath the surface, and I squeeze tighter, ignoring her whimper and the fear pooling in her eyes. What kind of person does it make me if I want to watch the life fade from her eyes?

Good? Evil? Bad? I haven't decided yet. See, I wasn't always like this. I used to love Kennedy, but now I'd rather watch her drown. While my sister had died that night, Kennedy was able to cover up the single scar she'd been given. Studying her closer, I notice the slight tremble of her body and enjoy that I'm causing her so much fear.

Backed into a corner with nowhere to go, I smile cruelly down at her. I'm a good foot taller than her, not that height matters. Trapped in my web, I could do whatever I wanted to her. She'd never be able to fight me off. If I wanted to break her open and see what's inside, I could. At the thought, my grip on her tightens, my fingers digging into her flesh.

"Jackson…" She gasps but doesn't make a move to fight me off.

Narrowing my gaze to her face, I inspect her as if I could figure her out with a single look. Maybe I can use having her here to my advantage. I can make her suffer, make sure that my sister gets the revenge she deserves.

Death would most definitely be kinder to her than I ever would be.

"It's your fault. All your fault, and now you dare come here… to Blackthorn?" The words claw from the back of my throat and out of my mouth as I pull her away from the wall just to push her back again.

The back of her head bounces off the wall slightly, and her hazel eyes bulge as if she didn't expect me to do what I just did.

It takes everything in me to not squeeze her throat any harder than I am. I want to hurt her, break her, make her feel my pain, and yet, an invisible rope holds me back, refusing to let me cross that line.

Why is she here?

"I didn't know," she whimpers, her entire body trembling. The last thing I want to hear is her excuses. Nothing she ever says will bring my sister back. Nothing will make all the wrongs right. We are trapped in this fucked up world together, and if it wasn't for Kennedy making such a stupid choice that night, my sister would be here. But she isn't, and because of that, I'm no longer the good boy with a heart of gold. I'm no longer kind and gracious. That guy died the day my sister did. Now, I take from women, and fuck and drink until I can escape the pain. The pain that she caused. It would be so easy to end this, but again my body refuses to let me.

"Shut up," I growl, leaning into her face.

My entire body is shaking now, and I don't know what I'll do next. Part of me wants to hurt her now, end it, but the rational part of my brain knows I could make her life worse in other ways. I could make her suffer, elongate her pain. It'd bring me more pleasure that way...

"Stop!" A scream pierces the air and fogs around my head. Shock splinters through both Kennedy and me at the sound. Turning to look at the newcomer, I find a woman, roughly the same age as us, and most likely a student here. She's staring, watching us.

Fuck. I know I have to let Kennedy go. This chick has seen me, and if I don't go now, I'll have to explain myself, and I'm not fucking doing that, so reluctantly, I release my hold on her throat and take a step back. My eyes remain on the unknown woman, who is watching me with a simmering rage in her eyes. I could tell the girl to go away, that everything is fine, but maybe this is fate's way of saying that's enough for today.

Clenching my fists, I force myself to take another step back, going in the opposite direction of where I want to go. Kennedy remains against the brick wall, her body shaking like a leaf in the wind. I've delivered my message, and hopefully, she'll take it, digest it and get the fuck out of here before it's too late, because if she doesn't... I can't even think of how badly the repercussions are going to be for her.

With one last lingering look at Kennedy's fear-stricken face, I turn and shove my hands into my pockets. I walk down the sidewalk like nothing happened and blend into my surroundings. I don't turn around or even glance over my shoulder as I walk. I doubt Kennedy is stupid enough to follow me, and that girl, what could she possibly say?

With every step I take, my thoughts become a little clearer, and my plot for revenge thickens. I won't convince her to leave, no, I'll make her stay. A smile pulls at my lips, but it doesn't feel right. Deep down, I'm not a bad person, but for my sister, for her memory, I'll be whatever I need to be. Kennedy had better watch her back because I won't just rip her to pieces. I'll destroy her, tear her apart, and watch from the sidelines with a smile as she begs me to stop.

2

KENNEDY

The nightmares find me like a beacon of light after my interaction with Jackson. Never in a million years did I think I would see him again. Least of all here. Not that Blackthorn isn't a good university to attend, it's just not one that I thought he would've chosen for himself. He always talked about going to Berkley, so how he ended up here, I don't know. Well, I kind of do, but I loathe thinking about it.

I do my best not to think of him or the way he looks at me. Angry, dark, and completely lost. My heart thuds deep in my chest. He hates me, maybe just as much as I hate him. I've always known that Jillian's death was my fault, but it was Jackson's fault just as much.

He should have been there at the party in the first place. If he would've been there, everything would have been different. She would still be alive... I would be... I can't finish the thought without wanting to vomit.

He looked just like he did the day I left, just more mature. His eyes the most vivid green, his mousy brown hair tousled like he ran his fingers through it. I could feel every hard inch of his body as he pressed me against the brick wall.

Thinking back on the other day and how I reacted, he probably thought I was scared to see him. Which I was, but only because I knew seeing him would bring up a plethora of unwanted feelings. I'm not scared of him. There is no pain he can inflict on me greater than the pain I'm already inflicting on myself.

Stop. Don't think of him. I feel myself slipping down the dark tunnel and into the abyss. The events of that night will never leave me, but I've learned that I can't hold onto them if I want to be present in the world.

I don't deserve to be here, but my therapist and parents are pushing me. Claiming it's time, time to move on, time to let go of the pain... *Time.* Such a funny word. Time couldn't heal wounds as deep as mine. It couldn't make the nightmares go away.

I make it to creative writing 101 early. The class is still empty, which means I get to snatch the best seats by the window. This is only the second week of classes, but I already love this class. Last week we discussed one of my favorite books, and since I love writing, the homework was fun instead of annoying. There is not much in my life that still gives me joy. Reading and writing are part of those very few.

Getting my reading material and notebook out, I go over my paper in my head. The teacher, Mrs. Jarrid, walks in shortly after, taking her seat up front. Students slowly filter into the class, but I barely pay them any attention, immersing myself in my paper. I make some final notes and changes when suddenly my hand stills, and the pencil tip stops moving across the paper mid-sentence. The fine hairs on the back of my neck stand on end, and my chest tightens.

"You heard me, move. I'm gonna sit here now." Jackson's dark voice pierces through the air leaving goosebumps behind on my arm.

I glance up and twist around, watching him settle into the seat behind me. The guy who was sitting there a moment ago walks away while shaking his head.

"What are you doing here?" I whisper over my shoulder.

Why the hell is he here?

"Oh, me?" he questions innocently. Leaning in, so only I can hear him, he whispers, "I'm just here to make sure your life is miserable." A sinister smile splits his face before he straightens back up, dismissing me completely. Turning back around in my seat, I feel the need to barf.

The class I loved last week becomes one I'm barely able to stand. It has nothing to do with the material or the teacher and everything to do with the person sitting behind me. I can feel his eyes on me, and even though he hasn't said a word or moved, I know he is staring at me, watching me.

My body is stiff and rigid as I sit in the chair, trying my best to make it through class, which is much harder than I ever could've imagined.

Twice, I almost got up and left. The only reason I stayed is because I wasn't going to give him the satisfaction of seeing me back down. No, I don't deserve to be here, but I am, and there isn't anything I can do to change it. My parents basically forced me to come here. I was perfectly fine where I was, but they wanted me to get out of the house.

I know Jackson hates me, but I hate myself far more than he ever will.

Trying to focus on the professor, I force my gaze to the front of the room, but I can't shake the heat against the nape of my neck. His tangy scent of lemongrass and citrus surrounds me, intensifying his presence ten-fold. How can he still smell the same after all this time?

I thought coming here would help me forget about my past, but with his stupid scent and presence, I'm reminded of a time when he held me in his arms, kissed my forehead and told me everything would be okay.

"You remember how much Jillian loved writing, don't you?" Jackson's whisper fills my ears and my entire body tenses at her name.

Jillian. If it isn't the loss of her that kills me, it'll be the guilt that I'm left with. It's like a fresh wound that never heals, even years later. It only seems to fester, never getting better. Every single time I think about her, there is nothing but pain, sadness, and guilt.

Refusing to acknowledge Jackson, I continue doodling on my paper while pretending that I'm not completely zoned out. I don't want to feel right now. Don't want to breathe or be here.

My fingers itch to inflict pain...

"What? Don't you remember anything about your *best friend*? Or is it that you just can't acknowledge the fact you killed someone? That you ripped a future right out from under her feet?" The pain in his voice cuts through me like a dull butter knife. I should tell him I'm sorry, but I'm not stupid. Sorry, won't bring her back. Sorry, won't take the pain away. He hates me just as I hate him. It's a double-edged sword that neither of us will escape without casualty.

I feel tormented, broken. I don't want to feel. Don't want to drown in guilt and shame. Curling my hand into a tight fist, I sink my nails into the meat of my palm. At first it stings, but then pain erupts across my hand, and something in my head clicks; it's almost like I get a high from hurting myself. It's a momentary second of silence before everything comes back down on me. Pain triumphs any and all other emotions, it swallows them whole. Pain is the only thing that shuts it all down.

I'm lost in thought when I feel Jackson's hand creep up the nape of my neck. Every hair on my body stands on end. Heat spreads up my chest and into my cheeks when I feel his hand circle the back of my neck. Squeezing as if my flesh is a stress ball, he leans forward in his seat. Hot breath fans against my ear, and even though I shouldn't, my body responds to the closeness of his.

"I'm going to enjoy watching you suffer. Watching you drown in your own misery. By the time I'm done with you, you'll be wishing it had been you that died that night and not my sister." A lump forms in my throat, and instantly, I'm drawn back into that memory.

Her lifeless body hanging there, vacant eyes, a future that she never got to have because of me. I was a killer. It was my choice to drive that night. I killed her. Killed us.

Squeezing my neck hard enough to leave bruises, he releases me with a shove, and I force a ragged breath into my lungs, not even realizing I was holding my breath.

"I'm expecting those papers to be done within the next three weeks," Mrs. Jarrid exclaims from the podium at the front of the room.

Like stepping too close to the sun, I can feel the heat of Jackson at my back, and I have to get away, get out of this room, get to my apartment, and release my emotions.

Standing abruptly, I bump my legs against the table, making a commotion as I shove my stuff into my bag. I know people are watching me, staring, but I don't care.

"Where are you going, killer?" Jackson taunts, but I ignore him. My shoe catches on the side of the table as I rush out of the room, but I steady myself before I eat dirt. I don't dare look over my shoulder. I don't want to see his sadistic grin or dark gaze that was once the one thing I looked forward to every day. I don't want to remember that he used to be my world.

I want to forget.

Escaping the room, I rush down the hall and burst through the double doors. The sun kisses my skin, and the air blows through my hair. I'm alive, but am I living? The thought comes from nowhere, and I push it away. I can't get my feet to move fast enough, and each step to my apartment feels like an eternity, my shoes weighed down with bricks.

A group of girls rush past me on the sidewalk, they're laughing and talking amongst themselves. Like normal college girls. I keep my head down and focus on the cracks in the sidewalk for the rest of the way to my small apartment. It's only a short walk to campus, and I got this by design. I didn't want to live in the dorms close to people, but I didn't want to live so far away that I couldn't walk. Since driving is out of the question for me.

Even if I hadn't lost my driver's license after the accident, I wouldn't have gotten behind the wheel again. I don't think I will ever be able to drive again, I can barely stand riding in a car in general. I've only gotten in a car with my parents since the accident, and I don't see that changing in the future.

I sigh when I finally reach my apartment and retrieve my keys from my pocket with a shaking hand. Relief is so close, close enough that I can almost taste it. Unlocking the door, I hurry inside and close it behind me before clicking the lock back into place. I deposit my stuff on the floor and rush into the bathroom.

My hands are shaking with anticipation as I pull my pants down and step out of them. I open the medicine cabinet and grab the tiny box where I keep the razor blades. With trembling fingers, I grab one and put the rest on the counter.

Sinking to the floor with my back against the tub, I look down at my thighs. There are countless scars that decorate my skin. Most are so tiny they are barely noticeable; some are bigger, and others are still red, raised, and healing.

I don't exactly know why I started doing this, but one day, I felt the need to do it. It started with nothing more than pushing the blade into my skin and later turned to deeper cuts. The rational part of me knows it's wrong to do this, but it's my one reprieve, for one second, I feel nothing, not shame or guilt, or fear. I might not know why I began, but I know that somewhere along the way, it morphed into something else... an addiction.

The one thing that helps me get through each day.

Holding the razor blade between my fingers, I bring it to a spot of unblemished skin and slide it across, watching as the skin separates.

Blood starts to pool along the blade, and my hand stops shaking, a euphoric feeling washes over me. The pressure on my chest is released, and suddenly, I can breathe again. Air enters my lungs rapidly as I suck in a deep breath and push the blade into my skin just a tiny bit deeper. Every time I do this, it becomes a little harder not to cut deeper, to stop myself from sinking the blade as deep as I can.

Do I want to kill myself? I don't know. What I do know is I'll do anything for five seconds of silence. Watching as the blood drips slowly down my leg, I feel satisfied. My vision becomes blurry, and my skin burns where the blade sliced through it, but it doesn't hurt. I think it should hurt, though all I feel is sated. Still, I need more.

Moving the blade a little lower, I cut myself again, sliding the blade across my skin. More burning, more euphoria... more silence.

Nothing can touch me when I'm inside my bubble. Not the memories. Not Jackson. Not the past. My emotions don't exist here. All I can feel is right now. Closed off from the world, there is nothing else that can reach me.

Inside here, I'm free, the pain I inflict on myself absorbs everything around me, making it possible to hold on for one more day.

One more day.

One more cut.

3

JACKSON

We all have our vices. Before my sister died, I was focused on my grades, on my future. I was a good kid. I didn't drink or fight. I didn't even smoke weed.

I had sex, but nothing like I do now. Using my body as a weapon, screwing any chick that bats her eyes at me. I used to be focused on being the perfect son and brother. Now, I focus on nothing but momentary pleasure. Anything that gets me through the day.

When Jillian died, a piece of me died with her. It broke off, shattered. My heart became a black hole for anger and pain. Now that *she's* here, I'm reminded of that loss and the pain. My anger is amplified.

"You sure you want to do this tonight?" Talon interrupts my thoughts. I met him during freshman orientation at Blackthorn. I wasn't trying to make friends, but the fuckface wouldn't leave me alone, and so here we are now.

Glaring at him, I continue stretching. "We're doing this, either that or I can pick some random prick off the street and beat the shit out of him."

Talon shrugs. "I guess. You know they have classes to deal with this shit, right?"

"What shit?" I pretend as if I have no idea what he's talking about.

Talon doesn't know me. He thinks he does because we fuck the same girls and have drinks together, but he doesn't *really* know me. He doesn't know the feelings I harbor, my past, the loss I've endured. He thinks I have an anger problem, and he's not wrong. I do.

But if he knew why I'm angry, if he knew what happened, then he would understand better. Problem is, I don't give a fuck about making him understand better.

"Why you always play stupid?" He grins at me.

Arching a brow, I reply, "Why you always ask stupid questions?"

Talon doesn't respond and just shakes his head at me. It's for the best, I tell myself. I'm not here for friends. In fact, I wouldn't be here at all if my mother hadn't guilted me into it.

Every Saturday night just outside of Blackthorn, at an abandoned warehouse, there is a fight. It's called the pits and for good reason, because two fuckers enter the "pit" and clobber the shit out of each other. At the end, there is only one winner. Most of the time, it's me, sometimes, it's some other fucker. I don't really care who wins, because at the end of the day I get my aggression out either way.

I guess you could say it's my personal version of anger management. Tonight there's only a small crowd. I look over to Franco, the guy who puts these things on, while I continue stretching, cracking each knuckle on my hand, as well as my neck.

The smell of sweat and smoke clings to the air. My muscles tighten at the mere thought of pulverizing one of these assholes' faces.

"You know the rules, fuckers. Tap out or knock out. Winner takes all the cash. We got a small crowd, but you better make it worth it for them tonight," Franco scolds as if we're elementary students who can't listen or comprehend basic rules.

Blocking him out, I scan the crowd, the girls are licking their lips, and batting their eyes as they look me and the other fighters up and down. We aren't seen as regular frat boys here. We're seen as sexed-up warriors, and these ladies want to take a bite out of us.

"Into the pit, you two," Franco orders, and I hop down into the makeshift ring, landing on the balls of my feet. I've ditched my shirt and am wearing a pair of low hanging shorts and tennis shoes. Sweat dribbles down my back and chest, my muscles tingle, and I lift my gaze, making eye contact with the guy across from me.

I'm going to fuck up his face tonight.

Grinning like a shark, I wait for the bell to ring. As soon as the sound pierces my ears, I take a step forward. The fucker in front of me does the same, but instead of sizing me up, he makes the first move, his fist flying through the air, and in the direction of my head.

Naturally, I duck and kick my leg out, taking him out at the feet. The sound of skin hitting skin is all I can hear, and it feeds into the adrenaline coursing through my veins. I feel high as I lurch forward and pummel the guy with my closed fists.

My knuckles make contact with his nose, and a sickening crunch meets my ears a moment before blood pours out. Even with blood coating my chest and hands, I don't stop. I can't. Each punch makes my muscles burn, and my heart thunder in my chest. Fuck, there is nothing better than beating the shit out of someone.

Focused on the fight, I don't realize two of Franco's men are pulling me off of him. He gets back up, and they release me. He's watching me, his eyes bleed into mine as he wipes away the blood from his lip. The crowd roars as Franco speaks into the microphone. Clenching my jaw, my molars grind together. The anger rippling through me is now at a low simmer, but it's still there, and I want it gone. *I want her gone.*

My lips curl at the thought of her, and I take a step toward the nameless guy. He follows, and soon we're slugging each other. I let him get in a few punches and kicks because the pain overshadows everything else, it dulls all the other emotions I'm feeling.

Fighting until we're both exhausted, I get the guy on the ground and pound his face in until he's screaming, his hand slapping against the ground over and over again. Then I stand and let Franco lift my hand, letting everyone know that I've won.

Climbing out of the pit, I'm greeted by Talon and two chicks I've never seen before. Their tits are hanging out, and they're wearing shorts that leave very little to the imagination.

I bet I could fuck them right here in front of everyone if I wanted to, and neither of them would object.

The brunette purrs, rubbing against me, placing her hand on my shoulder. "Let's fuck," she leans in, and whispers yells.

"Yeah, Jackson, won't you fuck us?" The brunette's friend adds, batting her eyes seductively at me. Rolling my shoulders, I shake the brunette's hand off me.

"No, thanks, babes, maybe later."

Both girls give me a pout but walk away on unsteady feet.

Running my bloody hands through my hair, I turn to Talon, who is counting out the cash that Franco just gave him.

"I need a beer," I grunt, already feeling the familiar ache in my muscles. There's a calmness inside of, me but I know a couple of drinks will make that calmness last a little longer, spread throughout my body. Slowly, my heart rate returns to a normal pace. Talon passes me a beer, and I pop it open and guzzle it down like water, crushing the can when I'm finished.

Fuck is that refreshing.

"Good fight tonight, Jackson. Maybe consider coming every Saturday?" Franco hints, just as he has been for the last month. He wants to highlight me as one of the main fighters, but I don't give a fuck about what he wants. I come here to let loose, mainly so I can make it through the fucking week without committing some type of murder.

My mom would be heartbroken if I ended up in prison.

"No, thanks. I'll let you know if I ever change my mind though." I sling my shirt over my shoulder and head for the door. Talon is hot on my heels, and I snatch another beer from him as we walk out to his car. The cool night air makes me shiver when it connects with my sweat-clad chest. Tipping the beer to my lips, I swallow down the frothy beer, letting the cold liquid cool me from the inside out.

Wiping my face with my shoulder, I crush yet another can and toss it over my shoulder once we reach Talon's car.

"Dude, you want to binge drink tonight or something?" Talon says, unlocking his SUV. His family has money, hell, everyone that goes to Blackthorn has money. Or grades. Good grades will get you in, it's how I got in, after all.

"I mean, it doesn't sound like a bad idea, but..." I pause as I open the car door and hop inside. "Actually, I've got a better idea."

"What's better than binge drinking?" Talon cocks his brow, and even in the dark, I can see the smile tugging at his lips. In a way, he's the devil's advocate, sometimes pushing me to do shit, while other times, he tugs me back away from the edge.

"Tormenting someone."

"What the fuck does that mean?" he asks, shifting the car into drive.

"It means I need you to take me over to Oakwood apartments."

"What's at Oakwood?"

"It isn't what but *who*."

"Sounds mysterious. Want to clue me in?" he asks, a little more curiously than I like. Do I want to tell him about Kennedy? *No.* My brain replies before I can even think about it. And not because I don't want him to know who she is, or because I'm hiding something. I'm not. I don't want him to know about her because I'm not ready for him to start asking questions, so leaving this entire thing open-ended is the best.

"Not really. It's no one important. I just need to stop by and pay them a little visit. Then I'll meet you back at the complex."

Twisting around in my seat, I grab another beer and open it just as Talon speaks, "You don't want me to stay and give you a ride home?"

"Nah, I'm fine to walk. It clears my head," I say before taking a chug of the beer.

I'm a lot calmer now. My head felt like it'd been run through a blender the last time I talked to Kennedy. Being so close to her, her scent surrounding me, having her so close but yet so far away. She's the only thing that I've left of my sister, and yet, I want to watch her burn. Want to see her bleed. No amount of pain I inflict on her would ever bring Jillian back, but it would make me feel better, and that's the best I have.

"You sure you don't want me to wait for you?" Talon says when we finally pull into the complex. It's late and Kennedy is probably asleep, but I don't really give a fuck. After following her home one night, I knew that I'd eventually come to this point. Showing up at her place, barging in. Briefly, I wonder if she'll fight me? Call the cops? Scream? The thought makes me smile. If she fights, I'll fight back, and I can guarantee it'll be the last time she pushes me.

"Jackson," Talon says my name, and I realize I never answered him.

"I'm good, man. Go home. I'll be a little bit." I chuckle as I open the door and slip out of the SUV. Tugging on my shirt, I close the door and wave Talon off. When he starts to back up out of the parking space, I walk to her apartment.

I know I shouldn't let my brain wander with thoughts of Kennedy, but it's hard, so fucking hard. There was a time when I cared for her so much, I would've ripped my beating heart out of my chest and given it to her, but then everything fell apart. She couldn't wait five fucking minutes. She couldn't wait for me to show up and take her and Jillian home.

Part of me wondered for a long time if things would have been different if I had been at that party that night and not fucking Nicole. Then I realized nothing I did would have changed the choice that Kennedy had made.

Making my way down the sidewalk, I cut across the grass and walk right up to her door. The screen door creaks as I open it, and I lift my bruised knuckle, banging on it loudly. If she was sleeping, she isn't now.

I keep my eyes firmly on the door and whistle a tune to stop myself from becoming impatient. A second later, I can hear the lock disengaging and the door opens, Kennedy's tiny frame comes into view, her face full of sleep. I let my gaze wander for half a second over her body, which is hidden beneath sleep pants, and a T-shirt that says "Book Nerd" in big, bold letters and hangs off one shoulder.

She looks adorable, but that doesn't change what I came here to do. Kennedy is going to pay, and the fun has just begun.

4
KENNEDY

I must still be asleep because there is no way that Jackson is standing on my threshold right now. And yet, there is no way this is a dream because if it was how could I smell him so vividly, see him.

My nose wrinkles at the assault of scents that greet it. Sweat, alcohol, aftershave, and... blood?

Peering up into his face, his glassy eyes meet mine. He's been drinking, and yet his movements are precise and without hesitation. I notice there is a small gash on his forehead, and his bottom lip is swollen and partially split open. *Was he in a fight?* My heart rate spikes at the thought. What happened to him? When I lower my gaze, my eyes find his hands, and I see that his knuckles are bruised, confirming my suspicions. Just another reason why he doesn't need to be here right now. Drinking and fighting. Yeah, I don't have time to deal with that.

"You need to leave," I tell him, my voice still laced with sleep.

His eyes pinch together. "I'll leave when I'm ready, thank you." Pushing the door open a little wider, he continues, "Why did you open the door in the first place?" He looks around my small apartment, which looks even smaller with his large body filling up the space.

"I didn't want you to wake up the neighbors," I say, a half-lie. That's part of it. The other part is I know it wouldn't matter. If he wanted to get in, he would.

"Sure, whatever you have to tell yourself, *bug*." I cringe at the nickname.

He used to call me Junebug when we were little as a pet name, but the way he says it now is filled with vengeful hate. It sounds more like an insult and not like an endearment that it was once upon a time.

Dropping my hand from the door, I take a step back. "What do you want, Jackson?"

"*I want* my sister back, but since I can't have that, I'll do with watching you suffer."

All you have to do is open your eyes.

How does he not see how much I'm already suffering? Have I become that good at hiding it? Or maybe whatever he sees isn't enough.

"Where is your bathroom?" he asks, scanning the room. I point in the direction of my bathroom, afraid that if I don't, he'll start opening and closing every door. Pushing past me, he waltzes through my apartment like he owns the place.

He flips on the light like he's always known where it is but doesn't close the door behind him. Instead, he starts opening the cabinets and drawers rifling through everything.

What the hell?

"What are you looking for?" I ask, my voice small. Does he need something? Pain meds? A band-aid, maybe?

He doesn't answer and continues rifling through my belongings like a madman. When he finds my pink makeup bag, he briefly stops and smirks at me over his shoulder before unzipping it and dumping its entire content out in the open toilet.

What the actual fuck? My mouth falls open, and for a while, I just stand there in shock. Why... Why would he do that? Dropping the now empty bag on the floor, he takes a few steps toward me. I'm intimidated by his presence, by his size. I don't know what to make of this situation. How did he even know where I was living?

Crossing his arms in front of his chest, he leans against the doorframe. It's a casual look for someone so menacing.

"You don't get to cover up your scar. Everybody needs to see what you've done. How ugly you are inside and out." His words are like a slap to the face, and even though there are many feet between us, I shrink back like he actually hit me.

"Fine, I won't wear makeup," I tell him after I compose myself. If that makes him happy, then so be it. I owe it to him to at least do whatever he wants or do whatever eases some of the pain that I caused. I don't really care what other people think of me anyway. The only reason I cover it up is so I can blend in better and stay off of people's radar. I don't want to draw any attention to myself, and I don't want anyone's pity.

Right after the accident, when my scar was still bright red and very visible to the world, everyone kept asking me if I was okay. Asking what happened and saying how sorry they were. I don't want to experience that again. I just want to be left alone.

"You've made your point. I won't cover my scar up anymore. Can you please leave now?" I ask, gesturing toward the door.

He cocks his head to the side and inspects me, his gaze roaming up and down the length of my body, and only then do I become aware of what I'm wearing.

The pajama bottoms cover every inch of my legs, but the T-shirt I'm wearing hangs off one shoulder and is tight across my chest, doing very little to hide my breasts. As soon as the thought enters my mind, my cheeks heat, and my nipples tighten. I'm sure he is well aware since his gaze falls to my chest, where the thin material of the fabric is showcasing my tits.

Wrapping my arms around myself, I cover up my boobs as much as I can, which only makes him smirk and draws more attention to myself. Embarrassed and completely defeated, I look down at the floor. Anywhere besides his stupidly handsome face will do right now.

"You know I turned down fucking two chicks earlier so I could come here. Maybe I should fuck you instead?" Shocked by his words, I look up again.

Our gazes collide, and he starts walking toward me. A low heat forms in my belly. I don't want to react to his nearness, but I can't help it. Everything about him reminds me of a past, of a life I no longer live in.

Closing the distance between us, he comes to a stop mere inches away from me. I can feel the heat of his body rolling off of him and slamming into me. I want to tell him to leave, to go away but the words won't come.

I watch cautiously as he reaches out and tugs at a piece of my blonde hair, rubbing the strand between two fingers as if he's testing its durability. It reminds me of a time when we were kids, and he'd always pull on my pigtails. Today that seems as if it was an eternity ago. What he just said finally hits me, and my response rolls right off the tip of my tongue.

"Why would you do that? You hate me." I don't know why I ask that question because once I say it out loud, I realize how bad it sounds. How much it sounds like I want that to happen.

"I don't have to like you to get off," he says, snickering, his eyes appearing darker.

"Well... I-I don't want to do that." I take a step back, desperate to put some distance between us, but he takes that as an invitation and instead moves forward, continuing to crowd me.

"I didn't want my sister to get in the car with you that night, but she did. Sometimes we don't get what we want..." His voice trails off, and I become increasingly aware of the fact that I'm alone with him in my apartment. He could easily overpower me, easily take whatever he wants from me. Would he really do that? Go that far? Would I even fight back? I'm not sure. I deserve everything coming my way, don't I?

Those vibrant green eyes of his twinkle with an unreadable emotion, and when my back hits the wall, panic starts to claw up my spine. I can't tell if he's trying to scare me or if he's serious when he moves even closer until there isn't even an inch of space between us. My chest rises and falls rapidly. Can he hear the thump of my heartbeat?

I'm trembling now, but I don't want to give away how scared I am.

He'll latch onto that fear, use it against me, wrap it around my neck like a noose.

Sighing, his hot breath fans against my face. "Are you scared of me, bug?"

"No," I murmur, only half lying. I'm not scared, not of him hurting me physically, at least. I'd welcome that... welcome the pain with open arms. What I don't want is to be reminded of the past, and that's all I can see when I look at him. I don't want those emotions to come back to the surface, not after I spent the last two years trying to drown them out.

"You should be," he growls like a dog, his teeth almost nipping the tip of my nose, and in the blink of an eye, his hand is at my throat.

His fingers wrap around it, squeezing, cutting off my air supply, making me gasp for air that will never come. Instinctively, I lift my hands and take hold of his wrist, trying to pull his arm away. Digging my fingernails into his skin, I can see the crescent-shaped indentations I leave behind. My lungs burn, and I struggle beneath his grasp.

Moving him is like trying to move a house. He is impenetrable and is only going to stop if he wants to. It doesn't take much to know that he's stronger than me, and he knows that.

Taking in the satisfying grin on his face, I would say he more than knows it, and he enjoys it as well. Enjoys the power he has over me. Even more shocking, I find that some twisted part of me enjoys it too. Being at his mercy, it... it does something to me.

"It would be so easy for me to end your life right now. I could strangle you with one hand. Stop your breathing and watch the life bleed from your eyes." His hold eases a fraction, and I part my lips, letting a frantic breath into my lungs.

I don't know why, maybe it's the lack of oxygen to the brain or the fact that I deserve his cruelty, that makes me say what I do next, but it puts into perspective just how dangerous Jackson is. Just how much he's changed and how far he's willing to go for revenge.

"Then do it. End me. We both know I deserve it," I croak, the words coming out labored.

The look on his face tells me I've just given him the ammunition he needs to end my life, and like a bull that's had a red flag waved in front of it, he charges. The hand at my throat tightens to the point of pain. My lungs shrivel, and the evilness in his eyes becomes terrifying. Instantly, I realize he will do this. He will end me, and I've put the thought in his head.

Squeezing tighter, my head starts to swim. I'm gasping for air that never comes, trying to push against him, to get him to release me. I'm only given a cruel smile in return and a harder squeeze. *He's going to kill me.* My vision blurs, and fear kicks in, but it's too late. I can't save myself just like I couldn't save Jillian that night.

I try to keep my eyes open, but it's hard, so hard... and then as if there is someone watching out for me, he releases me. I sag against the wall and bring a hand to my throbbing throat as air filters into my lungs again.

Tears slip down my cheeks, and fear slithers up my spine.

Jackson stands before me, his body shaking, his eyes gleaming with hate. He wants me dead, but more than anything, he wants me to suffer.

"Strangling you, though tempting, isn't enough for me. It's too sweet. Watching you suffer at my hand, watching you squirm and look over your shoulder in fear every day, wondering when I'll strike next. That will be worth it. Remember, I know where you live. I know where you sleep, and I hold all the power. If I want you dead, you will be."

His gaze roams over my body one last time, and then like a thief in the night, he turns and disappears out the front door. As soon as he's gone, I sink to the floor and let out a painful sob. The boy I once knew is dead, and in his place stands a cruel, sinister monster. I should've died that night. It should've been me, and because it wasn't, I'll pay the price.

5

JACKSON

I've become obsessed with Kennedy. I know her routine, where she goes for lunch, how much time she spends studying. I know she has no friends, which is only a little weird to me since she used to be surrounded by her peers.

Back in high school, she was popular, every girl wanted to be her friend, and every guy wanted to get into her panties... including me. Of course, I never acted on it, her being my sister's best friend, one of the many reasons. I didn't want to come between them, knowing how important Kennedy was to Jillian. Now I wish I had. Maybe my sister would still be alive if I did.

As I watch her more, I come to the conclusion that she lives a pretty shitty life, but she's still *living*, and that's half the problem. Lucky for her, she stuck to her word and stopped wearing makeup. I enjoy people staring at her face even though she doesn't seem bothered by it, which pisses me off. I was hoping she would be embarrassed, worried, that she would freak out when I poured her makeup into the toilet and told her she couldn't wear it anymore, but she surprised me when she agreed without a fight.

Shoving my hands into my pockets, I stalk after Kennedy. I don't think she notices me as I follow her to the library after her morning class. She's completely oblivious to her surroundings. One would think that you would watch your back more if you knew someone was after you, but she must not take me seriously. She must not believe that I plan to ruin her. Jokes on her because I'm going to drive the knife of pain deep inside her still-beating heart. She won't be able to do anything without knowing I'm watching, waiting to sink my claws into her again.

She walks through the double doors, bypassing the circular desk, heading straight to the English literature section, where she drops her backpack onto the floor and starts rummaging through the shelves.

Taking a seat at the other end of the spacious library, though still within view of her, I watch her from afar, getting a thrill out of knowing that she hasn't noticed me yet.

It's like a cat and mouse game we're playing. Right now, she is a carefree mouse, scurrying about without realizing that the cat is on the prowl.

Anticipating the moment she sees me, I rub my palms over my jean-clad thighs. I look forward to the shock in her face when she sees me, knowing that I will scare her, or at the very least, make her uncomfortable. Her eyes lift, and she looks away from the bookshelf.

I'm certain any minute now, she is going to look right at me but instead, she looks elsewhere, at a guy that's approaching her.

He's an athlete, wearing his Blackthorn Elite football jacket with pride. He smiles at her, and I can see his beady eyes moving over the length of her body. His lips are moving, but I can't make out what he's saying to her.

This strange, unwanted bubble of emotion rises within me. Jealousy? Rage? Why would I be jealous of this guy? If I really wanted Kennedy, I could have her. I could take from her and she wouldn't even tell me no, and yet, I can't shake the unwanted feelings away.

My hands ball into tight fists, and the carefree feeling I had moments ago swirls down the drain. Kennedy shakes her head, the blonde strands of hair catching in the morning sunlight that filters through the window, making them appear as if they're spun gold. I'm reminded of her sweet scent from the other night. Floral with a light dusting of something else.

She's a temptation. So beautiful, perfect, but a tempting poison that will kill you if you take a sip. The jock's face falls when Kennedy turns, picks up her bag, and walks away. Her shoulders are curled in, and she looks uncomfortable even though the guy didn't do anything but talk to her.

What the hell?

My brows pinch together with confusion. This is the kind of thing she likes, attention, guys falling over their own feet to get to her, so why is she walking away from him? It has to be a front. She's playing a game, being shy, pretending to be someone she isn't in hopes I'll get off her back, but that's not going to happen.

I can't and won't be fooled by some fake-ass mask that she wears. Does she forget that I know her? Really know her. My jaw aches as I clench it. The fact that she's turning this into a game pisses me the fuck off.

Pushing up out of the chair, I walk in the direction she went. Who does she think she is? Pretending that she doesn't want attention, that she isn't outgoing or a ball of fucking sunshine. As long as I've known her, all she's ever done is talk to people. She loved being the center of attention, both her and Jillian thrived from it, like goddamn plants in the summer sun.

There's no way she's changed that much. I might not see the whole picture when it comes to Kennedy, but I'm not stupid. She wants me to think she's changed. Well, it's time I show her which one of us actually has.

Speed walking, I catch up to her just as she passes the door that heads up to the stacks. An idea pops into my head, and I decide to go with it. Let's see how far I can push her before she breaks. She's basically jogging through the place as if she can outrun me. *Not today, princess.* Reaching out, I grab her by the shoulder, stopping her from taking another step.

A gasp slips past her pink parted lips as she comes to a halt and turns to face her assailant. Pain lances across her features as if struck at the sight of me.

"Jackson," she says my name in a hushed whisper, and I hate that it still has the same effect on me as it did the day before my sister died.

I wish every good memory I had with Kennedy would die. Every thought, every feeling. I wish it would all wilt away and become dirt beneath my feet.

"Don't say my fucking name," I grit out, reacting with venom as I release her shoulder and snake my hand around her wrist. Tugging her toward me and back to the door that leads up the stairs, I can feel the resistance she puts up, attempting to dig her feet into the ground and tug her arm out of my grasp.

"Where are we going? I don't want to go anywhere with you." The underlining panic in her voice only encourages me more.

Twisting the doorknob, I open the door and tug us up the first couple of steps.

"I don't really give a fuck what you want to do. I have a lesson to teach you."

"Can we not do this today?" Fear trickles into her nonchalant response as I pull the door closed, and darkness blankets us. "And how did you even know I was here? Are you watching me?"

A smile curves my lips, but I don't respond. Practically dragging her up the steps and across the expanse space, I stop when we're hidden behind a set of bookcases. Little slivers of sunlight filter through the dust-covered cases, but aside from that light, the entire room is dark.

Releasing Kennedy's wrist like it's fire, I reach for the button on my jeans.

"What...what are you doing?" Fear. It rushes off of her in waves. It's suffocating. Intoxicating.

Good.

I want her fear.

I want to taste it.

Feast on it.

"Downstairs, I realized something..." I trail off, flicking the button on my jeans. The sound ripples through the space between us, and though it's hard to see, there is no way I could miss the trembling in Kennedy's little body.

I try not to pay attention to how small and vulnerable she looks, or how wrong this is. I can have any girl I want, willingly, and I'm sure I could have Kennedy too, but right now, I don't want her willing. I want to take from her. Drink up her fear. Watch her break, and piece herself back together again.

"P-p-please, Jackson." Her pink lips quiver, and she lifts her hands as if she could fight me off. What does she think is going to happen here?

"I think it's time you drop the act. If you're trying to prove you've changed, that you aren't anything like the girl you used to be, you're doing a shit job at showing it. I can see right through it, and since you think this is a game, I'll show you how much it isn't by proving how much I've changed. How much I truly don't give a fuck about you."

Crowding her, I place both hands on her trembling shoulders and press down. Her body crumbles to the floor, and her knees land harshly against the concrete floor.

"No...no... I won't. I can't." She's shaking her head, and I ignore the real fear in her voice now. I shut down my emotions, my feelings, my need to protect her, over my need to ruin her. It's strange to feel two opposing emotions at the same time. Tugging my zipper down, I shove my jeans to my ankles and then my boxers, letting my hard, swollen cock spring free.

My emotions might be haywire when it comes to Kennedy, but my cock isn't. My cock wants her body wrapped around it, her cunt full of my semen.

Kennedy scurries back at the sight, and the first cry of fear escapes her lips. It's real and sounds more like a wounded animal.

"Come on, be a good fucking girl and suck me off. We both know you always wanted me to fuck you. You've wanted this since you were old enough to realize what it was, so let's do this." I take another step forward, and she lets out another cry, but this time, she rolls onto her side and pulls her body into a tight ball. Horrendous sobs fill the room, and I'm taken back by them. My entire body clamps up, and my cock deflates.

"Stop it! Stop this fucking show and get up," I yell at her, but she doesn't respond at all. For a few moments, I just stand there watching her fall apart at my feet.

What the fuck is wrong with her?

This isn't just fear. This is something else. Something that I'm not sure I can comprehend right now. Fear, I can handle, begging me not to do something, I can handle, but a complete and utter breakdown, turning in on yourself. I can't fucking do it.

Anger surges through my veins, and I'm confused about what I should do. Tugging my boxers back up and my pants, I button myself up before slamming my fist into the side of the bookcase. Fucking fuck. I can't break something that's already broken.

"You've been spared this time, but next time, I'm taking whatever the fuck I want from you. Tears or not, you'll feel the pain I feel eventually."

She sobs harder, and because the sound touches something inside of me, I walk away. The alternative is going to her and wrapping my arms around her, telling her that everything is going to be okay, but it isn't.

It hasn't been for a while, and it never will be.

Kennedy became the enemy the night she killed my sister.

6

KENNEDY

*I*t took me two days to return to a normal routine. I spent almost an hour in the library, trying to get myself to stop crying and calm down after the incident with Jackson. Then I dragged myself out of the building and went straight home, where I showered, scrubbing my body of the filth I felt before crawling into bed. Jackson couldn't have known what he'd done. That he recreated my worst nightmare.

I never told him, or anyone, for that matter. I never got the chance. After Jillian's death, my life became a blur of darkness. My own fears and the things that happened to me, no longer mattered.

It took months for me to stop wishing it was me who had died that day, and even now, I still think about how it never should've been her. Today is only the second day I've left the apartment since what happened in the library. I haven't seen Jackson, and my emotions feel as if they're balancing on a tightrope with shark-infested waters a few feet below.

Looking over my shoulder like a paranoid freak, I rush into one of the local coffee shops on campus, one because coffee is my weakness, and two because I needed to get off the street for a second before I had a mental breakdown.

I know it's only a matter of time before Jackson pounces on me again. Yes, I had a breakdown in front of him, and he saw me shatter, but I doubt that's going to hinder him from attacking again. I think my behavior surprised him more than anything, next time, he'll be prepared.

He's determined to make me feel the pain he feels. Even though I already do. I live in the pits of hell inside my mind. Nothing he does can be worse than what I already do to myself.

The Bean. That's the name of the place I just escaped into. It's quiet and has a warm, comfy feeling. There are small lounging couches, chairs, and tables, on the far wall are some bookshelves. I decide to give the place a try and walk up to the ordering counter.

"Hey!" A young-looking guy–who is probably a student here–pops his head up from beneath the counter, damn near scaring the hell out of me.

This shit with Jackson has me freaking out over every little thing. With my heart beating out of my chest, I force the words past my lips, "Hi, can I get a vanilla latte iced."

"Of course," he says, smiling, and I can tell from the look on his face that he wants to say more, but I'm not about making conversation. The old me would've sat here all day and talked to him, but I'm not that girl anymore. Plucking a five-dollar bill out of my wallet, I hand it to him with a smile and start walking toward the other end of the counter, where it says pick up. I do my best not to look at him and instead pull my phone out and pretend like I'm talking to someone.

How pathetic is my life? I'd rather pretend to be talking to someone than talk to the person directly in front of me. As I scroll through my phone, I navigate over to my call list and realize that my mother had called me when I was in my last class.

"Iced vanilla latte," the guy I tried to ignore calls. I step forward, claiming my drink while almost dropping my phone onto the counter.

"Thanks," I reply. He gives me a tight-lipped smile and walks back over to the other side of the counter to help the people standing there. Once again, I've let the chance of a conversation, of reaching out, of being a typical college-aged girl, slip through my fingers.

It's then that I'm reminded of something my therapist told me, *"Jil-*

lian is dead, but you aren't. You can't change the outcome of what already happened. You can only go forward. You have to move on. Let go. The past is the past, but you aren't going that way, are you?"

Would she want that? Would Jillian want me to let go of the pain? To move on? To forget what happened? She was such a kind person, always smiling, always helping someone. She was my best friend, and because of the domino effect of incidents, she isn't here today. Knowing Jillian, she would expect better of me, expect me to be happy and smiling, to carry on remembering her, and loving her, but she has no idea how much her memory hurts me. How much it hurts, because I am the reason she isn't here. Me. It's all my fault.

"Excuse me," someone mumbles as they pass by me, and it's then that I realize I'm still standing in the coffee shop. I need to get out of here. With my coffee in hand, I walk back out onto the now quiet street. Everyone should be in or near their classes now.

Everyone but me. I choose to skip creative writing today, even though it's one of my favorite classes. It's too soon to see Jackson's gorgeous but frightening face after what happened. Sipping the icy coffee through the straw, I'm met with a surge of joy. I don't once look over my shoulder, knowing that Jackson is in class right now, waiting for me to show my face and not following behind me.

When I reach my apartment, I walk in and toss my stuff onto the small sofa in the living room. The place starts to look more and more like a home every day. I both loathe and enjoy it. Locking the door, I slip off my sneakers and walk over to the couch, settling against the cushions of the sofa.

I have to call my mother back because if I don't, she'll call my old therapist, probably the dean of the university, before sending out a swat team or worse, she'll show up here. Entering the unlock code on my phone, I navigate to my call list and sigh as I hit the green call key.

The phone rings once, almost as if she's sitting right on top of it, watching for my call to flash across the screen.

"Hi, sweetie! I'm sorry if I interrupted you. I just wanted to check in and see how things are going. It's been a while since we talked."

I roll my eyes. "It's been three days, Mom, and I'm doing good.

Going to classes and enjoying living the college life." The lie comes easily since I'm used to telling people that I'm fine when I'm not. I think about the scabs on my legs I've been picking on and the new cuts right below. My mom can never know about any of those.

"I hope you aren't staying inside your apartment all day and night. Remember, your therapist said it was good for you to get out and socialize, meet new friends."

"Of course not. I'm really making an effort, Mom. I promise."

There's a rattling noise, and I swear when she speaks again, her voice is thicker, filled with emotion. "I can't tell you how happy that makes me. I was so worried about sending you off to college, but your father and therapist told me you would be fine. You've made so much progress. I wish I was there to see it."

I haven't, and I really don't want her here. I don't want her to find out how big of a lie this all is. How close to the edge I am. She'll make me come home, make me go back to the therapist every other day, and that's the last thing I want right now. Sometimes the best thing you can do is leave someone alone and let them navigate the dark waters alone. I don't want or need anyone else's help, least of all, my overprotective mother's.

"I know, but I'll be home to visit for the holidays, and then you can see. I promise everything is okay. I love and miss you."

"I miss you too. Remember, you can call us anytime. If you need anything or to just talk. I know your father isn't that easy to talk to, but he does love you and is proud of the strides you've made." I think that's a lie my mother tells herself.

As if us moving states away after the accident didn't hurt my father. He had to quit his job of twenty years and find work elsewhere. That night didn't just change my life, it changed everyone's lives. Everyone I cared about was affected by my actions. My father will never admit it, but he's ashamed to call me his daughter, and I don't really blame him. I'm ashamed that my heart is still beating most days.

"Yes, I know, Mom. Look, I've got to go. Study group and all, but I can call you in a couple of days. Okay?"

"All right. Please, be safe and take care of yourself, honey. I love you so much," she says into the phone. I don't say anything, and instead, hang up. The accident made my mother love me more, while it made my father resent me. All of that is okay, though, because the way they feel about me doesn't matter. I know I'm a killer. I know I did this to myself.

Taking another sip of coffee, I'm hit with a jolt of joyful pleasure as it reaches my belly. I shouldn't be able to be happy, even if it's from something as simple as drink or food. Feeling sick to my stomach, I walk into the kitchen and pour the beverage out, watching as it swirls down the drain.

Throwing the cup away, I walk back out into the living room. I'm feeling antsy, but I know if I start doing something, I'll feel better. My apartment is already spotless, so I pull my books out and start on some homework.

For about two hours, I work on my paper for economics class. I nibble on my bottom lip as I scribble down sentence after sentence.

The sound of heavy knocking on my door has me damn near falling off the couch. I know without even looking through the peephole who it is. I should let him assume I'm not here, but I guess I'm a glutton for punishment because I unlock the door and pull it open a little bit.

Jackson's stupidly handsome face greets me, but he isn't smiling. No, the look he's giving me promises pain and fear.

"You missed creative writing. I told the professor I would stop by with the assignment."

Wow. I'm a little shocked. It's unlike the Jackson that I've come to know now, but I give him the benefit of the doubt and open the door a little wider, extending my arm out for him to hand me the paper. My naiveté is almost laughable.

Catching me off guard, he shoves the door open, forcing me to take a step back as his hulking frame fills the doorway. The stoic look on his face gives way to a malicious grin, and I know something bad is going to happen. Fear snakes up my spine and tightens around my throat.

"You... you didn't come here to give me homework, did you?" I bite my bottom lip to stop it from quivering. Every time I'm alone with Jackson, I am reminded of how different he is.

How little he cares. It's shocking because the boy I remember would've killed anyone who looked at Jillian or me the wrong way. But I guess that boy died when she did.

"How did you know?" He grins, stepping all the way into the apartment, closing the door behind him. We're completely alone now. Yes, if I screamed loud enough, my neighbors would hear, but I'm not sure they would do anything.

"I don't want you here. Leave. You can't keep barging into my apartment. I'll go to the police." The threat doesn't meet its mark and only seems to piss him off.

In a second, Jackson has me cornered, his huge body towering over me, making me feel small and insignificant.

He leans into my trembling form and whispers into the shell of my ear, "Call the police. They won't help you. No one will. No one can save you."

"Please, just leave." I lift my hands out of instinct, mainly to push him away, but find the moment my hands touch his chest, the noise around me becomes a low hum. As if my touch burns him, he takes a step back, and my hands fall away, coming to rest at my sides.

"No can do. I've come to collect my payment. It's time to use that mouth of yours. My cock is only so patient." I swallow the scream of terror, trying to claw its way out of my throat.

"Jackson, please... please, don't do this..." The fear is so real. The memory of that night is all I can see inside my head. The way they held me down and used my mouth over and over again. I can still feel their hands on my skin, feel the saliva sliding down my chin.

"Such a fucking slut. You think Jackson can protect you?" Fingers dig into my head, ripping the hair from my scalp, still, no matter how bad the pain, I don't open my eyes. I refuse.

"Don't make this harder than it has to be, bug. All you're doing is sucking my cock. You owe me some fun, don't you think?" Jackson's voice pierces through the hazy fog around my mind, but every muscle in my body has locked up. Words refuse to come out of my mouth, and when he reaches for me, his hand grazing my shoulder, I wince and tuck myself against the wall.

"You want it rough, is that it? Do you want me to..." His words trail off, and his body comes to a standstill.

When I look up from the floor, I see his eyes glued to a spot on my bookshelf. It only takes me a second to realize what he is staring at. In a small pink frame is one of my favorite pictures of Jillian and me. It was taken on my thirteenth birthday. We were blowing out candles of my giant pink cake together. We did it together because she was making me laugh so hard, I couldn't do it on my own.

"You don't get to have a picture of her," he says, his voice is low and gravely, laced with so much hatred it's dripping from each word. "You don't get to look at her! You don't even get to think of her!"

Boots hit the ground heavily with each step as he walks over to the shelf. He grabs the picture and holds it in his hand. With his free one, he swipes the entire contents of the shelf off. Books, pictures, and knickknacks fly through the air before they can hit the floor, Jackson has already wiped out the shelf below.

He doesn't stop until the whole thing is cleared, and all my stuff is scattered out on the floor. Then he walks to the cabinet and continues his path of destruction there.

I just stand there with my back pressed against the wall. Invisible restraints holding me down. I feel like my feet are cemented to the floor, my body unable to move, even my lungs barely work. I don't think I've taken a full breath in the last ten minutes.

He continues destroying my apartment for what seems like forever. When he is finally done, he is out of breath and sweat covers his face. His eyes look dark, manic, and there's this profound hurt, so much hurt in those green orbs. I want to go to him. Wrap my arms around him and tell him how sorry I am, but I can't, nor would he allow it.

With a clenched fist, he takes a step toward me, but then as if rethinking what he wants to do, pauses. I wouldn't be surprised if he tried to strangle me again. There is so much pain rolling off of him. I doubt he would be able to stop this time.

"Don't you dare ever put up a picture of her again. You don't deserve to see her smiling face. You deserve death. It should've been you. It should've been you!" he screams, the sound splinters through me. For a long moment, he stands there staring at me like a bull ready to charge, and then out of nowhere, he turns around and leaves.

The door slams shut, and I jerk from the sound. Closing my eyes, I slide down the wall, my legs unable to support me any longer. My whole body shakes with each ragged sob that rips from my chest, and all I can do is wrap my arms around my legs and think of how right he is.

How it should've been me and not her.

7
JACKSON

*A*nother day of classes, and another night of misery. I thought the nightmares of not being able to save my sister had stopped, but it seems since that night at Kennedy's house, they've gotten worse. I do my best to avoid all thoughts of Kennedy, but it's hard when I'm doing everything in my damn power to make her life fucking hell.

I had every intention of making her give me a blow job when I went to her house, but that blew up in my face like a giant bomb of fucked up. When I saw that picture of Jillian and Kennedy, I was sucked back in time. The pain flooded into my chest, every ounce of it poured like rain from the sky, making it hard for me to breathe, and all I could do was react.

"Dude, what the fuck are you thinking about? Been getting pussy that's worthy of daydreaming about or something?" Talon pokes fun beside me as he shoves chips into his mouth.

I look down at the tray of food I got for myself. None of it looks appetizing right now.

"I'm not daydreaming, asshole. I just don't have anything to say."

"Sure, if you say so."

A group of girls walk into the cafeteria, their voices carrying across the room, and I cringe at the sound. It's like nails on a chalkboard.

Girls are good for fucking, but that's it. At least the ones I end up meeting. They aren't the type I would ever bring home to my parents. If my mom knew half the shit I did, she would have a stroke.

"Crystal is looking at you like she wants to take a spin on your dick." Talon elbows me in the side just as I lift my eyes, confirming exactly what he said. The girl looks like she wants to suck me off, right here, under the table.

I snort, "They all want to fuck me, what are you talking about?" Just then, Crystal and her group of friends start walking over to our table. Inside, I want to stab myself in the eye with a fork to avoid talking to her, but on the outside, I plaster on the smile that makes panties disappear and prepare myself to make her swoon. Maybe I can get her on her back to help take some of the ease out of my balls. All the taunting and bullying of Kennedy leaves little time for getting laid.

"Jackson, Talon," she greets us, batting her eyelashes. It looks like something might be in her eye, but I don't say anything. That's not going to get her to sit on my dick. Girls like assholes but only if they're half assholes, not full ones.

"Crystal, how are you?" Her face lights up with joy. I'd met her a couple times at house parties but only knew her by association, so I'm guessing she didn't expect me to know her name.

"Uh… I'm good. My girls and I were wondering if you were going to be at the party the football team is putting on?"

Talon and I exchange a look and shrug. "I guess it depends if you and your girls are going to be there."

Crystal licks her lips, and I bet she's picturing herself on my dick right now. Her friends are looking at me like they want to eat me too. Maybe I'll do a two for one special.

"Uh, duh, we'll be there." Crystal smiles, but it does nothing for me.

"Then we'll be there too, baby," Talon purrs.

The girls nearly clap their hands together like a group of kids excited for dessert.

"Okay, well, guess we will see you then." Crystal drags her teeth over her bottom lip, and fuck, she's trying to get me to chase her.

All the joy in the room deflates when I spot a blonde head of hair, that's connected to a slim body, walking into the room. It's not illegal for her to be in the university cafeteria, but it's not common. I've never seen her eat on campus.

Crystal and her friends are still standing in front of us, but now that Kennedy is here, those girls seem so mundane and plain. They are nothing in comparison to Kennedy, who is still the prettiest girl here, even without makeup and a scar on her face. I ban that thought from my mind as fast as it popped in.

Wanting to kick myself for even thinking about her like that, I watch her hips sway, her tight little ass looks so plump in those yoga pants.

Like a radar on me, she turns in my direction. Our eyes lock in a battle of wills, and as if she's seen a ghost, she drops the apple in her hand, spins around, and walks out of the cafeteria.

I can't help it. I smile. Mainly because I didn't have to do a damn thing to make her feel uncomfortable. Simply being here is enough to scare her away.

When she disappears from view, Crystal and her posse have taken a table about fifteen feet away from us. I can feel her eyes on me, watching me, but I don't look at her. Instead, I stare at the spot Kennedy was just standing at, almost willing her to reappear there.

"Who is that girl?" Talon asks, forcing me to look away from that spot and back to him. I contemplate telling him that she's no one, but it doesn't hurt anyone other than Kennedy if I tell him what really happened. The knowledge is out there, free for anyone that searches for it.

"Her name is Kennedy. She killed my sister."

"Wait... What? She killed your sister? How is she walking free? Shouldn't she be in jail?" The disgust in Talon's tone only encourages me to tell him more.

"She should be, but the judge thought otherwise. She got off with a slap on the wrist if you ask me," I sneer, doing my best not to remember that day in court. How distraught and heartbroken she looked. Fake, it was all fake to avoid jail time.

"How? How did it happen? I mean... you don't have to tell me if you don't want to. I just can't believe that girl killed someone. Like... murder?"

"Might as well have been. She went to a party with my sister. Both of them were drunk. They called me to pick them up. I was with a girl. I told them I would be there soon, but Kennedy didn't want to wait. They left, she drove the car and wrecked it halfway home. My sister was ejected. She died instantly." It kills me to even talk about it. My chest feels heavy, and the words come out slower. I hate that the last memory I have of my sister is telling her I would be right there and then not coming soon enough.

I was busy fucking some chick that didn't mean anything to me. I didn't even talk to Nicole afterwards. I should've been there for Jillian, but instead I was with another girl.

The worst part is that I only went out with Nicole to forget about Kennedy. I thought fucking another chick would get rid of the feelings I had. I didn't want to come between her and my sister so I did everything I could to get Kennedy out of my head. How could I have known that could've saved Jillian's life by doing exactly that.

"Fuck, man. That's... that's fucked up. I can't believe she is here, going to school and that you haven't murdered her yet."

I smirk. "It isn't without a shit ton of restraint, but yeah. So, now you know."

"I'm sorry about your sister. I know it doesn't help, but figured I'd say it."

"It's okay. She's gone, and I can't bring her back. Nothing to be sorry for."

"I know, but you're my friend, and I'd be an asshole if I didn't say it."

The feeling in my chest is too heavy. I need a subject change. I look down at my clenched fists, feeling the blood pumping through my veins, itching for a bit of violence.

"Call up, Franco. Tell him I want a fight. The bigger the guy, the better."

Talon raises his brow in question. "You sure about that? You took a pounding last time. I'd prefer if I didn't have to use a spatula to peel your body up off the bottom of the pit."

"Just do it. Tell him to set it up, and then spread the word around campus. Get everyone to come." I'm already giddy, simply thinking about it. Talon pulls out his phone even though he looks reluctant about doing so. I watch him type up a text and hit send, then I get up and grab my tray. Walking over to the garbage can, I toss my stuff into it and head back to the doors that lead outside.

"Where are you going, man? You didn't even eat," Talon calls.

"Not hungry," I tell him with a shrug and walk out the door without looking back.

Pausing for a moment, I stop to think where Kennedy may have gone. All her classes are done for today. Obviously, she came to the cafeteria to eat, and since she didn't do that, my guess is that she's most likely going home.

Starting in the direction of Kennedy's apartment, it doesn't take me long before I catch up to her. Her shoes slap against the wet concrete as she walks down the sidewalk like she is trying to outrun something. *Can't outrun me, baby.*

I follow closely behind but not close enough to draw her attention.

She maneuvers around a group of guys heading toward her, hugging the left side of the sidewalk, maintaining an even amount of distance between them and her. A light drizzle falls from the sky, making my shirt damp. The smell of rain surrounds me, and as we come up to a crosswalk, I see the red do not walk sign blinking.

Kennedy either sees it and doesn't care or doesn't notice. I don't know which one it is, but the only thing that matters to me in that instant is reaching her fast enough. A van barrels down the road, heading straight for her. My heart clenches in my chest, fear pulses through my veins as I see it happen in my mind. Acting without thought, I reach out before the image in my mind can become a reality. Gripping onto the back of her shirt, I pull her back just as her foot touches the lip of the curb.

The van races by, laying on its horn while Kennedy's back slams into my chest. Instinctively, I wrap my arms around her. Before I come to my senses, I lower my head and bury my nose in her hair. For a few seconds, I allow myself to inhale her sweet floral scent that's mixed with the smell of rain. Just this one time, I tell myself.

Shifting in my arms, she looks up at me, fear written in her features. I want to shake her for being so stupid. For not paying attention. Does she want to die? Why wouldn't she look up before crossing a busy street?

It occurs to me then that I could've lost her. I could've lost my last piece of Jillian. It makes me aware of the fact that, though not much, I do care about Kennedy enough that I don't want her dead.

"You saved me," Kennedy whispers, almost breathlessly. Her pink lips are parted, her hair is damp, and her cheeks rosy with embarrassment or maybe shock.

Snapping out of it, I release her. "Are you stupid? Why would you walk out into a busy street when the sign was blinking red?" I force the fear out of my voice and replace it with anger. It's not fake either. I'm furious. Why would she do that?

"I..." Her bottom lip trembles and tears well in her hazel eyes. I can almost see the old Kennedy in there. The girl I would do anything for. She's close, almost within distance, and yet so far away, I won't reach my hand out and grab her. I don't want to go there. I don't want to feel anything for her. I don't want to care about her.

Sneering, I take a step back. "Pay the fuck attention to what you're doing. I can't torment you if you're dead." Distance is what I need right now. I don't really care about her, it's just my sick obsession with getting revenge that has things twisted.

Kennedy exhales, her chest deflating. "What... What were you doing here? Were you following me?"

My lips tip up at the sides in a half-smile. "I'm always following you, Kennedy. Always watching you. Pay attention," I tell her one last time before shoving my hands into my pockets and walking away. I leave her standing there because the alternative isn't something I want to face right now. Kennedy can't matter to me. She can't become anything more than revenge. Not now, and not ever.

8

KENNEDY

I replay the moment in my mind over and over again. The van almost hit me. Just another step, and I would've been gone, my life over. I still don't know how I feel about it. For a long time, I felt like I should die, that I would do anything to trade spots with Jillian. I've never feared death. Instead, I've always hovered on the verge of welcoming it... until now. Since that almost hit the other day, I don't think I want to die anymore.

Even more confusing is the fact that Jackson pulled me away when I figured he would have been the one to give me a push. Why did he do it? Why didn't he just let me walk into the street? Isn't that what he wanted... me dead?

"That's it for today," Mrs. Bay says, dragging me out of my thoughts, dismissing the class. "Assignments are due next week. Don't be late because if you are, I'm deducting ten points for each day."

I grab my book and notebook and stuff it into my backpack before getting up from my seat. Walking out, I spot two girls who were sitting beside me in the classroom. They spent most of the class gawking at me and whispering to each other. I wouldn't be surprised if they were looking at my scar. I should be used to it, especially now that I've stopped wearing makeup, but I don't think I ever will be. The reminder of it all hurts too much.

Shaking it off, I walk past them and out the door, but not before I hear one of them say, "I heard she wrecked her car while driving drunk. Killed someone too."

"She should be in jail, not college..."

Their words steal the air from my lungs. How do they know about the accident? About Jillian? Pain slices through me, but I force my legs to keep walking. The ground moves beneath my feet, and suddenly I feel like I can't get away fast enough.

Holding onto the straps of my backpack with an iron grip, I start running down the hallway until I burst through the doors leading outside. I run and run until my lungs burn and my legs cramp up. Until I'm gasping for air, and my vision becomes blurry with tears. And even then, I continue running because if I stop, I'm afraid of what might happen.

~

I HAVE to force myself to go to my next class. At least I had four hours between my little breakdown and now. Even though I feel like my eyes are still puffy from crying, I walk into economics class with my head held high. No one seems to notice me as I walk in, which is fine by me. I don't want to draw any attention to myself. Taking the last seat in the back row, I pull out my book and notepad and set everything out neatly in front of me.

Grabbing my pencil, I tap it against my notepad anxiously.

I really don't mean to eavesdrop as I wait for the teacher to start the class, but when I hear Jackson's name come up in the conversation between two guys sitting a row ahead of me, I stop tapping the pencil and listen instead.

"Why would he fight again this week? He only had a fight last week, and he never does more than one fight a month," one guy says, searching through his backpack for something.

His friend shrugs. "I don't know, but I'm telling you, Jackson is gonna fight Boris tonight, Franco made a big announcement last night. I want to go just to see how crazy it is."

The first guy finds whatever he was looking for and slumps down into his seat. "Boris? That guy is huge, and he fights dirty. Brings knives and shit. Jackson is gonna get his ass handed to him. Fuck, he'll be lucky if he comes out of the pit alive. Boris is crazy, and he'll do anything to win." The pencil slides from my fingers and rolls off the table. I should probably bend down and get it, but I'm momentarily petrified.

Fear has its hold on my throat, making it hard to breathe. Jackson is going to get hurt. Why would he get into fights like that on purpose? Why would he put himself in danger like that? Doesn't he know all it would take is one hit to the head, and he could die?

Does he want to die?

The teacher starts the class, but my mind is somewhere else. I can't focus on anything that is being said. All I can think about is this fight that Jackson is going to be in with this Boris guy and how dangerous it all is. I know he hates me, and he has every right to do so, but I don't hate him. Maybe I thought I did. I wanted to, but I never did... I'm not sure I could, even if he scares me and tries to make my life hell. The last thing I want is for anything to happen to him.

I need to warn him.

Now the real question is, will he listen to me? I doubt it, but I have to try.

The class flies by even though I don't listen much to what is being taught. I'm too busy trying to figure out how to find Jackson. I don't have his number, and I don't know where he lives. I guess my only chance is to go to that place *the pit* and hope I catch him before it's too late. He'll either hate me more or thank me. Either way, it's a risk that I have to take.

When class is dismissed, I tap the guy in front of me on the shoulder. I try to hide how nervous I am when he turns, giving me a questioning look.

"Hey, sorry... I overheard you earlier. Ah... talking about the fight? Where exactly is that at?"

The guy raises a skeptical eyebrow at me, and for a moment, I don't think he is going to answer me at all. "The pit. It's in an old warehouse in the industrial park."

"Oh, okay. Thank you."

His friend has also turned around and is looking at me now. I can feel his eyes burning into my face.

"Want me to take you there?" the new guy asks, giving me a wide smile. "I'm going anyway, so it's not a hassle."

"Thanks, but I'm fine," I say while gathering my stuff up. "I'm not sure if I'm gonna go yet, it's not really my kind of scene."

The guy frowns. "It starts soon. You sure you don't want to come with us?" He's good looking, and obviously cares about his classes since from the looks of it, he's been taking notes all hour, but I don't want to make friends, much less get a boyfriend, and I know if I said yes, even for a ride, that's what he would think. That or sex, which isn't going to happen.

"No, I'm good. Thanks again," I tell him as I brush by him and speed walk out the door.

I remember seeing the industrial park on the map I studied when I first got here. It would probably take me a good hour to walk there, but calling an Uber or getting into the car with anyone who isn't my parents is out of the question. Cars are a hard no for me. I'd rather walk three hours than get into a car and drive thirty minutes.

I drop my backpack off at my apartment on the way, but I don't even stay long enough to eat. Grabbing a jacket, I walk right back out and in the direction of the warehouse.

It ends up taking me an hour and twenty minutes to get there. I wasn't sure if I would even find the place, but when I saw a shit ton of cars pulling onto the road and turning a few blocks down, I knew I was in the right place.

It takes me a little while to get to the door, but when I do, there is a line. The line moves impossibly slow, and by the time I reach the front, I find a big scary man blocking the entrance.

"Ten dollars." He extends his hand out, and I blink rapidly before reaching into my wallet and pulling out two fives. As soon as the money kisses the palm of his hand, he ushers me inside. Entering the warehouse is like being dipped in ice-cold water and tossed into a hot frying pan.

It's a complete shock to your body. The noise is astounding, and I nearly turn around and walk back outside. The only reason I don't is this incessant need to protect Jackson, which outweighs the discomfort I'm feeling. Discomfort is a momentary thing, but losing Jackson if I don't warn him, could be life-altering.

Moving through the crowds, I follow the sound of skin slapping skin. I reach the front, shoving past some girl in a barely-there shirt, and find that Jackson is already in the ring. My stomach falls to my knees, and my heart collapses in my chest.

Jackson is wearing nothing but a pair of shorts and sneakers. His muscular upper body is on full display, and if he wasn't in so much danger right now, I might gawk at his physic. But as it is, he's facing a monster of a man, who's raining his fists down on him.

Then his gaze collides with mine, and as if there is an invisible rope between us, I feel myself being drawn to him. I can see the anger filling his features. He doesn't want me here, but I don't care. Cringing, I watch as he barely misses taking another punch to the head.

Come on, Jackson. Fight. I can't lose you too.

9

JACKSON

My muscles are already burning, adrenaline courses through my veins. I need to do this to keep myself sane, to keep myself from losing my goddamn mind. It's so loud in the warehouse tonight, I can't even hear myself think.

Franco delivered on getting the biggest, baddest, scariest, motherfucker he could find. Boris is, well, a tank. He looks like he eats people for breakfast, and though he seems big and bad, my fists are faster, and my stamina is top of the food chain.

"Are you sure about this?" Talon yells over the roar of the crowd.

"Dude, stop being a pussy," I growl, tired of him always fucking with my good mood. He worries too much.

"Whatever. It's your death." He rolls his eyes and tosses a water bottle at me. I catch it mid-air, twist the cap off, and chug the contents before crumpling the bottle. The cool liquid does little to ease the heat rolling off of my body. I'm ready to get this done and over with.

"You asked, and we delivered. Welcome to the pits, everyone. Tonight we have the baddest, cockiest, motherfuckers I know going head to head. B-O-R-I-S! And J-A-C-K-S-O-N!" Franco drags out our names, and the crowd lets out a roar that's deafening. I bounce on the heels of my feet, sizing up Boris, who looks as if he's a brick shithouse.

It's going to take more than a couple punches to knock him on his ass. Especially when his fists are as big as my biceps.

A tingle runs up my spine. I'm not sure why, but it swirls in the pit of my stomach. Shaking the feeling off, I focus on Boris, he's big and bulky, which probably makes him also slow. He might be a giant, but that doesn't mean he has speed or a good fighting instinct.

My hands are wrapped in tape, but we don't wear gloves. I check the wrap one more time before I put in my mouth guard and walk out of my corner. As soon as I step into the ring, I step out of the warehouse. Mentally, there is nothing here besides him and me inside this pit.

It's easy for me to drown out the people, the cheers, and the voices. I push everything away, fears, guilt, and worry... it's all gone at this moment.

This is how it is when I fight. It's my one escape, the only time everything is quiet around me. My demons can't reach me when I'm inside the pit.

I don't even hear Franco ring the bell, but I know the fight has started when Boris rushes toward me, fist raised. He takes a giant swing at me, air swooshes across my face, but as I suspected, he is slow. I can easily move out of the way in time for the right hook.

What I didn't expect him to do is follow it up with a left jab.

His fist hits me above my left eye, and it hurts like a bitch. My head snaps back with the force, and I see stars. Jesus, fuck, he might be slow, but his fists pack a punch.

Shaking off the pain, letting it fuel me, I take a step to the side, avoiding his next punch. I need to be smarter and faster than this guy if I'm going to win.

Moving around him, I get in some good jabs here and there, but nothing seems to faze him. His pupils are blown out, completely black, which makes me think he's on something. He swings again, and I duck down, coming up with a right hook, my fist slamming into his chin. It's a hit that would have knocked most guys out on their ass.

This guy just smiles. *What the fuck?*

I'm so shocked that I'm momentarily distracted and don't see the next punch coming. His fist clobbers me in the side of the head, and I swear it feels like I got hit with a fucking brick. Before I can recover, he hits me again, this punch landing in my gut, knocking the air from my lungs. Pain lances across my body like a lightning bolt.

Trying to get away from him, I stumble back, but he continues his assault. Raining punches down on any part of my body he can get to. My head spins, and my stomach churns. I've never tapped out before, never had a reason to, or was afraid enough to, but I'm fucking close now. My pride can handle the hit. I'm stupid, but I don't want to die.

Boris swings and gets me again on the head. Pain erupts inside my skull as my head is forced to the side. My teeth rattle in my head, and my vision blurs, and for a moment, I think I'm knocked out. Darkness blankets my mind, but then I blink them open, and suddenly, I see her.

Kennedy.

Her eyes meet mine, and everything around me snaps back into place. The people, the warehouse, fucking Boris... and right there in the center of the crowd is Kennedy. Her eyes are wide with fear, her lips trembling, and all I can think is that she doesn't belong here. I need to get her out of here.

Another punch to the gut that sends whatever air is left in my lungs out on a gasp. It reminds me that I'm still fighting this monster. Deep-rooted anger rises up inside of me, filling my veins with newfound strength. I'm a volcano seconds from exploding.

I don't know why she is here and why it bothers me so much that she is, but I know I need to finish this fight, get to her and drag her the hell out of here.

Boris swings, but this time I sense it and dodge it, moving my head, and making him miss by an inch. Rolling, I move away from under him just enough to barrel a right hook on the corner of his jaw. His fucking face is apparently made of steel, but at least I caught him off guard. He stumbles back, and I use that small window of opportunity to give him all I've got.

My knuckles hurt, but I push it away and keep hitting him. Punch after punch, I strike him over and over again. Head, chest, gut, back, head. Anywhere I can hit him, refusing to let him get even one shot on me.

All it takes is one last punch to the side of the head, and he slumps over, his body falling face-first into the ground. Shocked, I stare down at him while Franco counts to ten, giving the fucking beast a chance to get up and fight again.

Thankfully, he stays down, completely unmoving. Sweat drips down my aching body, and all I want to do right now is get the fuck out of this ring, grab Kennedy, and leave.

As soon as I'm announced as the winner, I climb out of the pit and head straight for her. The crowd erupts around me, threatening to swallow me whole, but I push through the masses to get to her. People rush past her to get to me, almost shoving her to the ground to congratulate me. Anger ignites deep in my gut, and when I reach her, I wrap a hand around her wrist and tug her to my chest.

The way she's looking at me, like a helpless little bug, it makes me want to save her and squish her at the same time. There is way too fucking much going on around us. I can't think straight.

Heading for the doors, I wrap an arm around Kennedy and drag her along beside me. Once outside, I can think, breathe, my mind becomes less foggy, and I drop my arm from Kennedy and instead take her wrist into my hand.

Her small legs can barely keep up with me as I practically run across the parking lot toward my car, wondering how and why she came.

"How the hell did you get here? Did you drive?" I ask. I've never seen her drive anywhere, but that doesn't mean she doesn't have a car. The other option is that she came with someone, and if that's the case, it better not have been a guy. Because if she came here with some dude, I'll kill him.

"I walked," she announces. *She walked?* That's, that's like five miles.

"You walked here? All the way from campus?"

"Yes, took me a while, but I did." She sounds almost proud.

"Why? Why the fuck did you come here?" Better yet, how the fuck did she know where the pits were and that I was going to be here.

Talon. Talon was spreading the word about the fight. She must've overheard someone talking about it. That still doesn't really explain why she was here though.

When she doesn't answer, I speak a little slower, "Why-did-you-come-here?" I'm tempted to shake the answer out of her. I'm tired of her making stupid choices and putting herself in danger, a danger that she acts as if she doesn't see.

"I–I... well. I overheard someone talking in class, and they said you were in danger. So... I came here to warn you."

The words trickle slowly into my brain, almost like I'm having a hard time understanding them. "You're fucking joking, right? What do you think this is?" I motion between us.

"Nothing. I just... nothing." Her face falls, and her eyes drop to the ground. "I shouldn't have come here. This was a mistake."

"Damn right, you shouldn't have, but now you're here, and you're coming with me," I tell her, and unlock the SUV with my keypad on the door.

"I'm not going anywhere," she replies, her voice stronger now, "and I'm definitely not getting into a car with you."

Of course, she isn't. I roll my eyes and open the passenger side door with my other hand. "Get the fuck in, or I'll put you in. I don't care if you want to ride in a car with me. Your fears are not my fucking problem."

My patience is thin as fuck, and if she doesn't decide in five seconds, I'm going to choose for her.

"Please, Jackson..." she pleads, but like I said before, my patience is good as gone.

Picking her up, I place her ass in the seat and strap her in with the buckle. She struggles for half a second before I pull back and slam the door.

Walking around the car, I climb into the driver's seat and grab the key from the center console. I start the vehicle, and the engine roars to life. Strangling the steering wheel, I throw the bitch into reverse and pull out of the parking spot. Tires spin and gravel flies as I shift to drive and rip out of the parking lot.

Glancing over at her, I see her fear-stricken face. Her hands are in her lap, where she is nervously playing with the zipper on her jacket. I wish she would calm the hell down. She has nothing to be scared of, at least not while I'm driving.

I'm not even sure why I give a fuck about her? She's nothing but a means to an end, really. Revenge and nothing else. Yet, I saved her life the other day and had this intense need to protect her tonight. I don't understand why I'm feeling this way, and it's annoying as fuck. I want to hate Kennedy. Need to hate her. Wanting or feeling anything else is a betrayal to my sister.

Halfway to my apartment, Kennedy speaks.

"Where are we going?"

"My place," I say through clenched teeth.

"What happens when we get there?" she asks, her voice meek.

"What do you think happens?" I shoot back.

"I... I don't know."

She doesn't know. Ha. What a fucking liar.

I don't reply, and instead, wait to say anything till we pull into the parking lot of my complex. Finding a spot, I put the car in park and kill the engine.

"You're coming inside with me," I tell her. She's coming inside willingly, or I'm forcing her. That's the only choice she gets in the matter.

"Why?" she asks as if she doesn't already know.

Leaning across the console, I inhale her sweet scent. She smells like flowers and fear, and fuck my cock is hard already.

"You know why," I say before forcing myself out of the vehicle.

Kennedy takes a minute to get herself together but climbs out as well, walking around the car to meet me. It's time for me to settle the score. It's time for Kennedy to pay the piper.

10

KENNEDY

*A*s I step into his apartment, all I can think of is what he said in the car.

You know why.

Yes, I know why he wants me to come in, but how am I going to get it into his head that it's not happening? I'm not giving him a blow job. *I can't.* I'll do anything else, but not that.

Walking closely behind me, Jackson closes the door once we're both inside. His spacious living room suddenly seems smaller, like the walls are slowly moving toward us. The space is surprisingly clean for a college student.

"I'm gonna take a shower, and when I come back, you'll be on your knees ready to suck me off—"

"No! I won't. Either we have sex, or I'm walking home." I shock myself saying the words out loud, but even more surprising is that I'm not scared. I'm not scared of sex with Jackson. I'd rather do that than anything else.

I've never actually done it, but when I was younger, I thought about him being my first. I imagined him taking my virginity, even touching myself at the thought of it. So, I'm definitely not scared of sex, I'm more worried about him turning me down.

When he doesn't answer right away, I look back at him over my shoulder. I'm not really sure what I expected to find when I looked at him, but the shocked expression on his face is new. I guess he didn't expect me to say that either.

"You want me to fuck you?" he questions in disbelief.

The tone of his voice changes. It's lower, almost breathless, and it has some weird effect on me. I feel hot, like the temperature in the room has suddenly risen by ten degrees. There's a tingling in my belly, and a heat creeps in that I've never felt before as I feel Jackson take a step closer. His scent surrounds me, and I feel a calmness wash over me. I can breathe, feel... the weight on my chest isn't so heavy right now.

"I asked you a question, bug. Is that what you want? Do you want me to fuck you?" he repeats, and all I can do is nod because the apple-sized knot in my throat won't let a single word pass. Before I can change my mind and tell him no, he is on me. His muscled chest bumps into my back, and his fingers wrap around my upper arms as he shoves me forward and into the room.

Oh, god, it's really happening.

"Fine, I'll fuck you," he growls venom in his words as he bends me over the back of the couch, pushing my face into a pillow. This isn't how I imagined this would go the first time, but I'm not about to try and stop him. Keeping one hand between my shoulder blades to hold me in place, he uses his free hand to pull down my yoga pants and panties in one go.

Cool air hits my exposed center, and I realize that I'm already wet. My cheeks heat and a shiver runs down my spine as I anticipate what's going to happen next.

Is he really going to do it? Is it going to hurt? Will it feel good? I wonder if I'm wet enough or if he plans to touch me?

All these questions swirling in my mind come to a stop when I feel his fingers between my thighs. Gently he strokes my folds, moving his fingers to my clit. Rubbing tiny circles against it, pleasure, like I've never experienced before, erupts from the tiny bundle of nerves, and I have to bite my lip to muffle a moan.

"You're already wet for me, bug," he says, his voice is so low and soft, it's barely recognizable.

He never talks to me softly anymore. Everything about him now is harsh, domineering. Leaning in, he presses his chest against my back, molding us together, letting me feel his erection on my naked bottom. He's still wearing his shorts, but the thin material doesn't do much to hide how hard he is.

"How long have you been thinking about me fucking you?" he questions. His voice is barely above a whisper now, but the words are enough to make more moisture form under his touch. The truth is, I've thought about this for a long time. Wanted it since before everything fell apart. It was always going to be Jackson, always. I wanted him to be the one to take my virginity. Jackson doesn't wait for my reply.

Maybe he knows I'm past words, or maybe he doesn't care to hear my response. I don't know. What I do know is he pulls away, his fingers between my legs disappear, and a moment later, they are replaced with the smooth tip of his cock.

"Are you on birth control?" he hisses through his teeth, sounding as if he's barely restraining himself.

"Yes." I sigh as he rubs his swollen tip through my arousal.

Guiding himself back to my entrance, I force a ragged breath into my lungs. The mushroom head of his cock feels huge, bigger than I expected. I get the feeling this is going to hurt, but I embrace the pain, welcome it. It's better than the sadness, the heartache. Anticipation clings to my bones, but I don't have to wait long.

Skimming his hand down my back, he enters me with one hard thrust and tears through my virginity with ease. He buries himself deep inside of me until his heavy balls press against my ass. Pain rips through me, and I whimper into the pillow, my hands clawing at the cushion as if it could save me from him. I feel like I'm being ripped in two, my insides shredded. Tears prick at my eyes, and I bite my lip to stop myself from screaming.

"Fuck, you feel good," Jackson grunts behind me, his hands on my hips as he plows into me over and over again.

His strokes are hard, powerful, and they hurt, fuck do they hurt, but beneath the pain is a sliver of pleasure. It sneaks in between each stroke like a thief in the night, and I want both, need both. Feeling impossibly full, I hold on for dear life as he fucks me with primal, raw rage. He's trying to imprint his hate on me, and I feel it. Feel every fucking lash as if he's beating me, the belt hitting my skin, and leaving a mark behind.

Fingers dig painfully into my hips, and I know there will be bruises by the time we're done. Heat blooms deep in my stomach, and slowly I loosen up, opening like a flower in full bloom. Jackson's balls slap against my clit with each punishing stroke, and it's enough friction to leave me panting, leave me craving more.

"I hate you," Jackson growls, releasing my hips, and moving a hand into my hair. He grabs a fistful of hair and tugs my head back, making my neck ache with the angle. My scalp burns, and for a moment, I am catapulted back to that night, the feeling too familiar.

No, no... I don't want to think about that. Not now, not ever. This is Jackson, not him... I wanted this, asked for it. I force the ugly memories away and concentrate on the here and now. On Jackson. I can smell him all around me, his citrus scent. I am here. Not there.

He releases his hold on my hair, and I let my head fall back down, face-first into the couch cushion. He grabs the back of my neck tightly, so tight it hurts, but it also brings me intense pleasure as he fucks me with every ounce of hate he has.

"I hate you so much. Why did you have to do it? Why? We could've been more than this... I could've..." His words cut off, but the animalistic tone of them pushes me closer to the edge, and the pleasure trickles in slowly, building at the base of my spine.

"Please," I beg unsure of what I'm actually asking him to do.

"You want to come? Come on my cock? You think you deserve that?"

"No. Yes. Please," I gasp into the cushion. My lungs are burning, my entire body is a giant knot of pleasure building up to the breaking point. I can feel my juices dripping down my thighs. I want this. Need it so badly, I might die if I don't get to come.

"Lucky for you, I really want to feel your pussy strangle my cock." I can practically see the sinister smile on his lips as he swivels his hips, hitting a spot deep inside of me. It's like being struck by lightning, every hair on your body stands on end, and you wonder if your heart might stop beating for one second.

"I..." Words try to escape me, but nothing comes out. My entire body tightens, my pussy clamps down on his cock so tightly I'm surprised he can still move inside of me.

Light forms behind my now closed eyes, and my entire body shakes as an orgasm rips through me, stealing the breath from my lungs. The pleasure is so intense, all I can do is sag against the sofa while Jackson uses my body. Aftershocks of pleasure tingle down my spine.

"Jesus, I'm coming," Jackson warns as he explodes deep inside of me, his sticky warm release painting the inside of my womb. I wish I could see his face, see the pleasure overtake him, but we aren't lovers, we aren't even friends. We're enemies, two broken souls floating through life, the results of a complete and utter tragedy. I knew what he was going to say to me a little bit ago, that he could've loved me, but that was the problem here, wasn't it?

He could've loved me. He just never did. Part of me knows that if he was there that night, Jillian would still be here. I wouldn't be broken, and neither would he. If only he would've loved me then, maybe things would've been different.

Something inside my chest fractures, and suddenly I'm overwhelmed with guilt and shame. The pleasure can only fog your brain for so long before reality comes crashing back through. This never should've happened. I know before he even pulls out that this was a mistake. Doing this with him has only complicated things further. I should be running away from him, not letting him fuck me on his couch. Tears start to form in my eyes, and bile rises up in my throat. I need to get out of here, leave, run away as far as I can, and never look back.

11

JACKSON

My body is flooded with endorphins, floating on a cloud as I pull out of her. I don't think I've ever come so hard in my life. I'm literally weak in my knees as I take a step back and look at Kennedy, still bent over the couch. With her perfectly shaped ass jutting out and her warm, wet pussy nestled between those creamy thighs, she is a sight to be seen. I could get used to seeing her like this. When I notice my come leaking out of her, my cock roars back to life.

Shit, I could fuck her again already. Looking down at my cock, I'm about to grab the iron rod when I notice something else. Mixed in with the glistening wetness of her arousal is... blood. It's not much, almost as if she was...

"Fucking Christ, were you a virgin?" My question gets her moving, but she doesn't answer right away. She pushes herself up from the couch and pulls up her panties and yoga pants frantically. Only when she is dressed, does she turn around. Her hair is a tousled mess, her cheeks a soft pink, and her eyes are filled with tears. She's looked thoroughly fucked and sedated. If it wasn't for the fucking tears in her eyes, I would say she looks pretty happy about it too.

"Does it matter?" Her question catches me off guard. *Does it?* Fuck, I don't know. It shouldn't, but I don't know how to feel about this. I just didn't expect her to be. She is nineteen for fuck's sake. Who stays untouched for that long nowadays? What the hell was she waiting for? Marriage? Prince charming? Well, she got neither.

"Yes, it mattered. If I had known, I would have turned you around, so I could see the pain in your face when I took this part from you."

For the first time since we started this game of hate and revenge, I see something that looks a little like anger in her hazel eyes.

"Fuck you, Jackson," she grits through her teeth.

Gesturing to my cock, I snicker. "Looks like you were the one that got fucked, so get your shit and get the fuck out." Tugging my shorts back up, I watch as she winces when she moves.

God, I'm an asshole. This takes the cake on all the shitty things I've done to her so far, but I know worse will come. I'm not done making her life miserable, not by a long shot.

She leaves my house, and though I don't look at her face, I know there are tears in her eyes. I can hear her sniffling, trying to hold back the sobs that will wreck her the second she walks out the door. If I had a heart, I might've cared. I might've called an Uber for her, so she didn't have to walk across campus. I might've done a lot of things, but she knew the score when she came here. She knew what would happen, and I can't feel sorry for someone who walks into something expecting a different outcome. I didn't promise her shit. Didn't even ask for sex. I asked for a blow job. Well, maybe not asked, more like demanded. She offered sex up herself, so the only person she has to blame is herself.

When I hear the front door close with a soft click, I get up from the couch and lock the deadbolt, then I head to the bathroom for a shower. My entire body is one massive ache, and as I turn the shower on and step under the stream of water, a terrible feeling overcomes me.

My stomach churns and tightens, and I feel like such a fucking dick. Hating Kennedy is my life now. I'm consumed with my need for revenge. She took the only other person besides herself that mattered to me. She killed my twin. Hating her is the nicest thing I can possibly do.

Washing my body, I'm overwhelmed by the fact that even if I don't want to admit it to myself, I still care. It's why I didn't push her into traffic that day, why I couldn't actually go through with forcing her to give me a blow job.

Clenching my fist, I lash out at the tiled wall with rage. My teeth grind together, and I hate myself a little more for not being able to fully hate her, for there being a morsel of care beneath it all. Why? I just want to hate her, to forget that she ever mattered to me, and yet every time I look at her, I see the little girl who hugged my sister on the first day of kindergarten. I see my sister's best friend hugging her. I see someone that should've protected her, instead of harming her, and maybe that's half the problem. I never should've expected that from Kennedy.

Punching the tile a couple more times, my knuckles are a meaty mess as I get out of the shower. Blood drips all over the pristine white tile, but I don't give a fuck. Drying off, I walk into my bedroom and pull on a pair of shorts. As soon as I step out into the hall, I hear a knock at the door. Gritting my teeth, I stop at the front door. I swear to god if it's Kennedy, she is going to wish she didn't show back up here.

My patience to deal with her is non-existent at this point, and though I don't want to physically hurt her, I'm toeing the line between right and wrong at this point. Unlocking the deadbolt, I tug the door open, a barrage of words cling to the roof of my mouth when I find it isn't Kennedy at all, but Talon.

"Hey, fuckface, got out of there fast enough," he says, shoving into my apartment. Fucker wants to get punched in the face, doesn't he?

"What the fuck do you want?" I whirl around to face him, slamming the front door since I already know he isn't going to be leaving right away. I'm not really in the mood for company tonight. I'd rather drink myself to death at this point.

"Is that any way to greet the person who comes with twenty-five thousand dollars in his pocket for you?"

My face deadpans. "Just give me the money, jackass. I'm not in the mood for company tonight."

Talon wiggles his eyebrows at me. "Oh, really? Is that why you ran out of the pit and to that chick? I saw her walking down the street on the way over here. Did you fuck her?" I don't say anything, mainly because there isn't anything to say. I don't have to tell him who I fuck and don't fuck. Does he think he's my dad or something? Agitated, I roll my shoulders. It feels like I'm being interrogated.

"I'm going to take your silence as a yes since you aren't denying it." He smirks. "Did you at least make it hurt? She deserves some pain after the story you told me. Hell, you should've kept her here, maybe I could've fucked her too. Made sure she got the point."

I don't understand my reaction to what he's said, but I pounce, grabbing him by the front of his shirt. "Don't fucking touch her! She's mine. Do you hear me? Don't touch her. Don't look at her. Nothing."

"Jesus, dude." Talon tries to push me off, but my grip on him is too tight. I'm tempted to rearrange his face, but I hold back. I've hurt enough people tonight. "I heard you loud and clear. Don't touch the blonde. I got it."

I release him with a shove, and he stumbles back. The shock over my outburst is written all over his face, and I don't want to see it. I'm ashamed to be feeling this way. I hate Kennedy, fucking hate her so much, it's all I can feel sometimes, but every once in a while there is something else, something deeper. It comes out of nowhere and makes me think twice about what I'm doing to her.

"You okay, man? You're acting weird," Talon says, pushing me to my limits. His voice is a saw cutting through me. I want to flatten him.

"I'm fine. Now get the fuck out of here before I beat the fuck out of you. I want to be alone," I yell at him, pointing to the door. He backpedals, his entire face ashen now. I can't imagine how I look at this point. Like a beast that's ready to explode.

Slamming down onto the couch, I take my head into my hands and listen for the door to close. When it slams shut, I shove up from the couch. Her fucking scent is all around me. It's in my head, under my skin. I hate her. I fucking hate her. There is no room for anything else inside of me. Walking into the kitchen, I grab the bottle of bourbon off the top of the fridge, twist the cap off, and bring it to my lips.

My muscles quake as I tip the bottle back and let the liquor pool inside my mouth before swallowing it down. It burns a path of fire deep into my belly, warming the coldness inside my chest. Tears prick my eyes as I sag to the floor and continue drinking.

"Why the fuck did you do this to me, Jillian?" I scream into the empty space.

It's not her fault she died. It's not her fault that she got into the car that night. It's mine. It's Kennedy's but never hers. She didn't deserve to die. I drink some more, letting the brown liquid cloud my mind, but nothing can truly make me forget. This is a temporary fix. Tomorrow, I'll wake up and be reminded of it all over again. Such a vicious fucking cycle.

"I hate her so much, Jill. I hate her, and I don't want to care, but a part of me does, and it feels like a betrayal. She killed you, took you from me..." I sob, feeling the loss of my sister for the first time. I never cried at her funeral. I couldn't. I needed to be strong. For my parents, for myself. Plus, crying wouldn't fix anything, wouldn't bring her back, but not allowing myself to mourn—my best friend, my twin, my other half—only made the emotions I was feeling ten times worse. I held it all in, thinking I could swallow it down, but all it did was swallow me. I was drowning, and there wasn't a lifeboat in sight.

Sighing, I down the rest of the liquid, and when it's empty, I toss the bottle at the wall, watching as the glass fractures, flying in a million directions. I'm not sure how many shards of glass the bottle has become, but I imagine that's what my heart looks like now.

It'll never be whole again.

Feeling the unbearable rage building inside me again, I want to hurt someone, but like always, there is no one here to hurt but myself. Needing to unleash the pain, I rear my hand back and punch the wall. One hit isn't enough, and neither is two.

I clobber the wall like it's the pain I face every day. I beat my fists into the drywall until I'm sure someone is going to call the cops, until my knuckles are bloody, and there is nothing left inside me. No anger, no sadness, just a numb feeling that washes over me, taking all the good and bad with it. Tonight I realized something... Kennedy might have been the one to kill my sister, but I helped. I helped put her in the ground. I'm to blame too. Sagging against the floor, I close my eyes and hope that I never wake up, that the nightmares become my reality.

12

KENNEDY

*I*t's been a week, and I still feel used. Like I whored myself out. I don't want to see Jackson again or think about what we did. It was wrong. We shouldn't have gotten pleasure from each other's pain, but somehow, we did. Immersing myself in classes, I focus on schoolwork and nothing else. I pick up a bunch of extra credit and toss myself headfirst into the work.

It's the only thing I can do to stop myself from thinking about him. Any time that my mind starts to wander, it's to him. I think about how angry he was and how he felt inside of me as our bodies became one. Thank god, I haven't seen him since that night. I'm not sure what I would do, or even say if I did.

As I rush from the library–with three books for my extra credit project in hand–I nearly collide with another person. Looking up from the ground, I prepare myself to apologize, only to realize that I know the person I just ran into.

"Oh, hey!" the girl says. I rack my brain, trying to remember her name.

"Hey," I mumble back, noticing that we aren't alone. There are two men with her, hovering around her like protective animals. Both are brooding and dark, with a possessiveness in their gaze. Is she with both of them? Are they her friends? I shake the thoughts away before they can take root. I don't care. I'm not interested, at least not really.

"Remember me? I'm Stella." She smiles, and her eyes twinkle with excitement. She's way too eager to make friends.

"Uh, yeah..." I press my lips together. I don't really want to do this. Not today, or tomorrow, or ever really. I don't need or want friends, but for some reason, I can't bring myself to tell that to this girl.

"It's funny that we meet again. Maybe we can go get a coffee or something? Or even have a glass of wine sometime?"

All I can do is shake my head and backpedal. "I... I don't think that's a good idea."

One of the guys she's with places his hand on her shoulder and gently pulls her toward him. "Let's go, Stella. She doesn't want to make friends, no matter how adamant you are." The smile he gives her is one of love and admiration, and I'm only a little jealous. A frown appears on Stella's face as she brushes some blonde hair from her eyes.

I feel bad, like someone kicked me in the stomach, but I still turn around and rush back to my apartment. I'm halfway to my complex when I realize the streets and quad are much fuller than usual.

"I can't wait to show you my dorm and the library. You're going to love it, Mom," a girl exclaims as she walks past me, a middle-aged couple following behind her.

Oh, god. Pressing a hand to my forehead, I can already feel the onset of a migraine. I continue down the sidewalk, and that is when my reality becomes a nightmare because of all the things I could forget, family weekend definitely shouldn't have been one of them.

"Kennedy!" my mother squeals as she runs down the sidewalk, wrapping her arms around me. "We called, but it went straight to voicemail. I wasn't sure if you still wanted us to come, but since we hadn't seen you in a while, I figured it would be nice to make the trip," she says as she pulls back. I gaze at my father over her shoulder. He hasn't moved an inch and doesn't look like he's happy to be here either.

My mother takes my clammy hand into hers and walks me toward my father as if I'm a small child that can't do it on her own.

"Kennedy," my father greets in a monotone voice. He used to tell me he loved me, that he was proud of me. Now, he barely acknowledges me.

"Hey, Dad," I mumble back.

"I got you a dress, sweetie. I want you to wear it to the dinner they're having for us tonight. Your father has to work on Monday so we can only stay tonight. We're gonna make the best of the time we have together."

I force my lips into a smile. It almost hurts, definitely feels strange and wrong because I'm not even close to being happy.

"Thanks, I'm so happy you guys are here. I need to head back to my apartment and drop off this stuff, then we can do whatever you want."

The next twenty-four hours are going to be pure torture, but at least it won't last forever. Soon enough, they'll leave, and I can get back to my life, or what's left of it.

"Of course. Let's go," Mom exclaims, and I want to groan, but bite back the sound. If one thing is off, this could turn into so much more than a weekend from hell.

"Let's," I reply and start walking toward my apartment again.

~

IT TAKES FAR TOO long to get my mother to leave my apartment, and by the time we do get out, it's too late to show them around Blackthorn because the dinner party is starting soon.

With each step I take, I worry about the dress my mom made me wear riding too high up my thighs. It's not terribly short. It sits above the knee, but only a few inches higher is where my scars begin. I don't want anyone to see those, least of all, my parents. God, they would ship me off to the next loony bin in a heartbeat.

"I don't understand why you couldn't have put on a bit of makeup?" my father says under his breath as we walk inside that banquet hall. His remark both hurts and angers me. It's obvious when he says put makeup on, he's asking me to cover my scar, so I don't draw any attention to us. Or, more so, to him. It's been clear to me for some time that my father cares more about himself than me. Ever since the accident, I've been more of a nuisance to him than a daughter. He is ashamed of me, and he doesn't miss a chance to show it.

My stomach lurches into my chest when we walk into the event, and I see how many students and parents are inside. I'm tempted to turn around and run back to my apartment, but if I do that, my mother would question me, and my dad would have yet another reason to belittle me.

I've told her I've been working on being more social, working on getting outside my bubble. I'd be giving myself away if I tried to leave now.

"Let's get a table," I say and tug my mother in the direction of an open table. She's bubbling over with excitement while I'm drowning in misery. Guess things never change.

"Kennedy, is that you?" I know that voice. The softness of it. For a long time, Jillian and Jackson's mom was like a second mother to me. I can't tell you how many times I slept over at their house. How often she made me pancakes or bandaged up my scraped knees. Still, seeing her after what I did, all those good memories are tarnished by the one bad thing I did.

I really don't want to turn around because I know Mrs. Wislow isn't alone. Her husband is here, and Jackson is definitely here. This is slowly becoming an actual living nightmare.

Building up the courage, I turn around and come face to face with Trish. Her eyes become glassy when she sees my face, and she rushes toward me, wrapping her arms around me as if I didn't kill her daughter. As if there isn't tons of misery and pain between our two families.

"Kennedy," my father calls my name sternly, but I'm an adult now. Not some kid that can be pushed around. If I want to hug Trish, then I will.

"You look good," she says, pulling away, her emotions written all over her face. It's stupid of me, but I chance a look around her and find Jackson's green eyes feral and honed in on me. He's not even bothering to cover up his disdain of me. "I'm so happy you're here and going to school."

"We'll be at the table, sweetie," my mother leans forward and whispers into my ear. I can't see my father's face since my back is to him, but I'll bet he looks close to murder. He and Jackson probably have matching facial expressions.

"We... We don't have to do this," I tell her, the wounds of my past becoming raw as she stands before me.

Ken, her husband, walks up to me as well, leaving Jackson to stand alone, his arms crossed over his chest, a sinister look flickering in his eyes.

Trish wipes away a couple stray tears that have escaped her eyes. "There is nothing to do, honey. Ken and I, we just, we had tried to reach out to you before, but your parents said you moved away. We wanted to let you know that we forgive you." She places her hands on my shoulders as if she knows I need the weight to hold me to the ground.

"You... you forgive me?" I'm shocked. That is not how I envisioned this would go.

Ken nods, his eyes are soft, and the same color green as Jackson's. "Jillian loved you like you were her sister, and we know you loved her too. We've come to terms with the fact that it was a horrible accident, and sometimes things happen that are out of our control. We miss her every single day, but hating you, or being mad about it isn't going to change that she's gone. Jillian wouldn't have wanted us to treat you that way. You're like a daughter to us. Losing Jillian wasn't a choice, something out of our control, but we can control our relationship with you."

Tears fill my eyes, but I blink them away. I will not cry. Trish smiles at me, and her smile reminds me of Jillian's. She was always so happy, even when everything looked like it was headed south, she made the best of a shitty situation. She was smart beyond her years.

"I thought you would hate me forever," I manage to whisper.

"Oh, sweetie, we are sorry, and I'm sorry we didn't come to the trial. At the time, we were just too hurt and grieving too heavily to go," Trish pauses, "we lost Jillian that night, yes, but we didn't lose you, and we kind of forgot that at the time."

My throat tightens. What do I say to that? I can't even get my brain to form a coherent response. They shouldn't be apologizing to me. I should be apologizing to them, and yet my tongue feels like it's weighed down with concrete.

Somehow, I get a response out, "I... I'm so sorry. I love you both, and I loved Jillian so much. I miss her every day. Every single day," I tell them, damn near breaking out into a sob. Forcing myself to breathe, instead of falling face-first into my emotions, I slowly get myself.

Trish's lips quiver, and I know she wants to cry too. "I would love to have lunch together sometime. Catch up? I want to hear all about your life since you disappeared with your parents."

Again, I'm shocked. "I... I don't know if that's a good idea." For some stupid reason, my eyes cut to Jackson, who is staring fiery holes through his parents and me. His mother turns and looks over her shoulder, discovering what I'm looking at.

"Don't let him scare you. He's still mourning her loss. He doesn't know how to deal with pain. Someday, he'll find a way to heal, but until then, he's going to be grumpy," Trish says, snickering. "Life is short, and losing Jillian taught us that."

"Would your parents be okay with us all sitting together?" Ken asks.

"Uhh, I don't know. I mean, they can't tell you to leave the table if that's what you mean."

Ken laughs, and it reminds me of all the times he would tell us stupid dad jokes, and he, Jillian, and I would laugh until our cheeks hurt, and tears rolled down our faces. I miss smiling, being happy, feeling joyful instead of dead.

"Good, then let's sit together," Trish exclaims and grabs my hand. Together we walk back toward the table while Ken turns and goes to talk to Jackson. He returns a moment later, shaking his head, and Trish gives him a little frown before shrugging her shoulders. My own father refuses to look at me as well, but my mother makes small talk with Trish.

It's awkward and uncomfortable, but it's the most structured my life has felt since losing her. Slowly, everything around me melts away, and I allow myself to feel normal for once. I allow myself to feel like I'm not the reason she died.

13

JACKSON

*H*ow can they do this? How can they talk to her like she didn't take Jillian from us? How can my mom hug her like she didn't destroy our life? How can my father forgive her as if it wasn't all her fault?

I've never felt so betrayed in my life. My own fucking parents, what a joke.

Sitting in the corner of the large room, I tighten the grip around the glass of champagne. My hand is shaking with barely restrained anger, and I know the thin glass is going to give way any second now. It's going to shatter in my hand, like my life shattered the night my twin died.

Even though it physically hurts me to do so, I can't look away. Every time my mom's hand rests on Kennedy's shoulder, I want to throw my glass at them. With every smile they give, it only adds gasoline to the fire. Fueling my hatred and anger until it threatens to swallow me whole. Darkness is my best friend, and I feel the need to give in to it right now.

They act like I'm not even here, ignoring me like they should be doing to her. I can't fucking take this any longer. I need to get out of here, I can't breathe.

Just as I get ready to walk out, I notice Kennedy getting up as well.

She heads to the bathroom, and instead of leaving, I decide to follow her. Taking the long way around, I avoid my family all together and make it to the bathroom just as she is walking back out.

Sneaking up behind her, I grab her by the arm and pull her back. She lets out a shriek and twists in my hold. "Jackson!"

"Shut up!" I keep dragging her with me. She stumbles over her high heels, and I have to pull her up before she hits the ground. Once we are hidden around the corner, in a corridor away from the event, and any prying eyes, I push her up against the wall.

"What fucking games are you playing? Trying to get close to my family again? What's the plan now? Killing someone else close to me?"

"What? No... I didn't mean for any of this to happen."

"You like playing the innocent little girl, don't you? You might be able to fool my parents, but never me, do you understand? I know what kind of person you are. I know how black your soul is. You're ugly inside."

"Stop! Let go of me, Jackson." Kennedy fights back, anger flickering in her eyes, which only fans the flame of rage inside me. If I wanted to, I could hurt her–really hurt her–but I wouldn't come back from that, nor would my heart allow me to do such a thing. No matter how much I try and deny it, I care too much about if she's living or dead, even though I shouldn't.

But there are other things I can do to her, other ways to show her that I'm in control and that I always will be. Sliding a hand beneath her dress, I grab onto her thigh, squeezing it harshly, making sure she feels me. I can give her pain if I give her pleasure at the same time.

Her eyes go wide, the hazel really standing out, and her throat bobs as she struggles to get away from me, but I push her back against the wall. As my fingers run up the inside of her thigh, she goes stone cold, and then I feel it. Something rough and raised against the creamy smooth skin of her thigh. I run my finger across the line, it feels almost like a scab.

"What is this?" I ask, reaching for the hem of her dress, ready to inspect myself. As soon as our eyes connect, I see the pure panic in them. She completely freaks, becomes this wild animal, hell-bent on escaping me. Her hands lash out, and her nails dig into the skin of my face as she drags them downward.

"Don't ever touch me again," she screams as she shoves at my chest, panic clawing its way out of her. I reach for her wrist but miss, and she comes back, landing a hard slap across my face. I'm stunned, shocked by the violent action, which gives her the moment she needs to shove by me and escape. Running away, she disappears while I hold a hand to my burning cheek, wondering if everything that just happened was a dream.

What the fuck was that?

She acted like I was going to kill her. I've threatened her before, grabbed her, and touched her without asking. She's never reacted like that before. *No.* This was different.

Whatever it is, it's big. She is hiding a big fucking secret, and I'm going to find out what it is.

I don't know why I stand there moping over it. I don't care what the fuck is wrong with her, just so long as she doesn't die because her misery is my enjoyment, and if she's dead, well, there goes my fun.

Waiting a little longer before I reappear in the banquet hall, I give myself a moment to get my shit together. I go into the bathroom and check my face in the mirror. There is a scratch mark across my cheek, but I can't do shit to hide it. Not going to lie, the fact that Kennedy attacked me is surprising as fuck.

Cleaning myself up as best as I can, I leave the restroom and walk back into the party. I make it all of two feet inside the door before my mother is on me, her face a mask of fury.

"What did you do to her?" my mother asks sternly.

I choke on my laughter. "What did I do to her? Do you see my cheek? She fucking attacked me. Plus, I'm not the one out here pretending like everything is fine and dandy." I take a step back, my voice rising, drawing attention from bystanders.

I don't care who sees or hears what I have to say. I'm past giving a shit now.

"I know you're hurting, son, but you need to calm down. It was an accident. Kennedy didn't mean to do it."

I hate how calm she sounds, how dismissive to what happened to Jillian she is. Her voice is like ants crawling all over my skin, and I want to sink my nails into my flesh and itch.

"An accident is running into someone with your shopping cart. Spilling a glass of milk. What she did wasn't an accident. It was murder and the fact that you can't see that..." I clench my fist, ready to punch something, someone, anything. I'm boiling water, that's bubbling over. "The fact that you can't see that makes you a fucking disgrace. You don't forgive the person who killed someone you love. It's disgraceful and shitty, and you're..." I back away needing to go somewhere else to escape this turtleneck of an event.

"Jackson, wait," my mother calls after me with tears in her eyes, but her tears mean nothing to me, not when she can sit with the enemy and pretend that everything is all right. Not when she'd rather talk to the person that killed her daughter than her own son, who is drowning right in front of her.

I don't wait.

I run, and I don't stop until my lungs burn, and my muscles ache. Until all I can do is pass out from exhaustion.

14

KENNEDY

The feelings are back, and I'm like a rock sinking to the bottom of them. He felt them, my scars, his fingers ran along the jagged, raised edges. He knows my secret, and he could tell anyone, my parents, his parents.

"What's going on, honey?" My mother intercepts me as I come rushing around the corner. All I could think was to get away from him, to make sure he didn't learn my secret, but that failed. He knows something is going on even if he doesn't really know what it is.

Forcing myself to calm down and pump the breaks, I wipe away the tears from my cheeks and pretend as if all is okay. "I'm just really emotional right now and having a rough time after seeing Ken and Trish, that's all. I think I want to go home."

"We just got here though," she says, frowning.

"You guys can stay if you want, but I feel sick. I'm going to go back to my apartment. Maybe we can have breakfast in the morning?" I try to lighten the blow of me leaving, and it must work because she smiles at me and gives me a hug.

"I would love that. I'll call you in the morning, and we can see what's going on." She releases me, and I nod. I don't bother saying goodbye to my father, it's not like he cares anyway.

"Tell Ken and Trish I'm sorry that I had to leave, please."

"I will let them know. Go home and get some rest. I love you," she says and then turns around and walks back to the table. Standing there for a long moment, I realize that I could be screaming for help in the open, and she would never see it. Not because the evidence isn't there but because she doesn't want to see it. Unless I tell her flat out, she'll never acknowledge it.

Needing to leave before Jackson shows his face again, or worse yet, opens his mouth, I walk back to my apartment, making my feet move as fast as they can without sending me to the ground. I try not to think of the anger I saw in Jackson's features.

His hate for me grew in an instant. He thought I was making nice with his parents when he had no idea that I had nothing to do with it. It was all on them but telling him that wouldn't change what already happened.

My chest aches, and I want to shut off the emotions I'm feeling. I thought maybe I was heading in the right direction, but Jackson ruined it all. He just had to touch my scars. As soon as I get into the apartment, I lock the front door, strip out of my clothes, and walk into the bathroom. Getting out the razors, I wonder if there will ever be a time when I can get through the emotions without needing pain. Pain covers it all up, it swallows all the sadness.

Plucking a razor from the container, I sit against the tub, spread my legs, and pick a spot to cut. My hand is trembling as I lift the blade and press it into my skin until blood beads against the edge of the razor.

Relief floods my veins as soon as I drag the razor across my skin, cutting through my flesh like a hot knife through butter. Euphoric pleasure pulses through me, and soon silence settles over my chaotic mind.

I'm back in my bubble, protected, sheltered from the storm of emotions. Making another cut, I hiss as the skin separates and a burn zings across the inside of my thigh. I'm not ashamed here. I'm not broken or sad. I am merely me. I drop the razor blade and let the endorphins consume me, feeling the warmth of blood against my thighs, and smelling the coppery tang as I breathe through my mouth.

After sitting there for a long while, I get up, clean the cuts, and wash my face before getting myself ready for bed. I feel lighter, free, and as I crawl into my bed, I consider talking to my parents about leaving Blackthorn. If I'd known that Jackson was here, I'm not sure I would've chosen to come here.

Still, if it comes down to staying here or going home, I'm staying. At least here, I don't have to deal with how much my father hates me or face the fact that my mom would rather ignore my problem than help me.

There is always the option of transferring somewhere else, but I doubt that would happen midway through the semester. I may just have to deal with Jackson for a little while longer. I can do my best to avoid him and hope for the best.

~

THE NEXT MORNING, I get up early and meet my parents at a local diner near campus. I'm both happy and sad that they're leaving today. Happy because my dad hates me, but sad because they are still my family, and at least my mom pretends to care about me.

When I walk into the diner, I find them sitting at a horseshoe-shaped booth. They've ordered coffee already, and one for me as well.

"Good morning, sweetie," Mom greets as I slide into the booth, taking the seat beside her. Dad doesn't even look up from the paper he's reading. I really don't want to react; I just want to push my anger toward him down, but I'm tired of being treated like garbage every time he sees me. I'm still his daughter.

"I ordered you a coffee, eggs, bacon, and toast with strawberry jam. I hope that's okay."

I nod and pour some cream and sugar into my coffee, stirring it with the spoon. Taking a sip of the coffee, I let it warm me all over before I set the mug down.

"Are you feeling better today?"

"Yes." It's the truth. I'm feeling much better today, but only because I cut myself last night. I always feel better afterward. It's like I'm cleansing myself when I do it.

"Good. We stayed for a little while longer and then went back to our hotel. Trish and Ken were sad that you left without saying goodbye. I told them you weren't feeling well."

Taking another sip of my coffee, I try not to feel guilty for walking out without even saying goodbye. They poured their hearts out to me, told me they loved me and missed me, and I disappeared to use the bathroom, and never came back.

"Personally, I'd prefer if you kept your distance from them. We just got settled into this new place. I don't want the past to get brought up all over again," Dad adds, finally glancing up from the paper. He doesn't look at me as he speaks though, more like through me, as if I'm not even there. I curl my hand into a fist beneath the table.

"Trish wants to have lunch, surely that isn't dangerous," I mock.

"I don't care if it's dinner, lunch, or a party. I don't want you spending any time with them. You killed their daughter with your underage drinking and driving. You're lucky we knew the judge. Otherwise, you would be in prison right now." And there it is. He always finds a way to bring me down, to make me feel lower than dirt.

Looking away, I say, "I'm starting to think I would rather be in prison."

"Oh, stop it, sweetie," Mom interjects, obviously, trying to defuse the situation. "Everything is looking up. Plus, you seem to be doing well at Blackthorn. College is just what you needed."

"Yeah, about that…" I fiddle with my silverware. "I was wondering if maybe there was another option. Maybe a different school I could attend. I like Blackthorn, but I'm…"

I don't even get to finish before my father interrupts, "You're so goddamn ungrateful. First, we make sure you don't end up in prison and help you so you can afford to attend this school, and then you ask if we can find you somewhere else to go."

"Travis," Mom scolds, her cheeks turning red.

"Don't bother, Mom. I don't know why Dad doesn't admit that he's ashamed to have me as his daughter. He'll never let go of what I did. He'll always hold it over my head, reminding me of how shitty of a person I am."

"Kennedy," she says, sighing. I can see how torn she is. She's being tugged in both directions, but I don't need my mom to take my side. I know I fucked up, but I don't need to be reminded of it every day.

Scooting out of the booth, I can see my mother wants to reach for me, but I shake my head at her. "I'm going home. You guys don't have to come here anymore. Clearly, Dad doesn't want to see me, and I'm done feeling like shit. Done being treated like this. I know what I did was wrong. I know I fucked up, but I can't change it. I can't fix this."

"Wait, Kennedy, don't leave, you haven't even eaten yet."

Almost laughing, I say, "You're more concerned about me eating than what I just said, and that is one of the problems, Mom. I love you, but I can't do this anymore."

I leave the diner with tears in my eyes but hold my head high as I walk down the sidewalk.

When I get back to my apartment, I make myself some breakfast and crawl back into bed. My fingers move all on their own, tracing over the scars, each one a reminder of how close I was to breaking. I've survived so much so far, surely, I can survive Jackson a little longer.

I'll just avoid him, just like I'll avoid my parents. I'll live in my own little bubble and hide from the rest of the world. Either way, I'll survive because something tells me that's what Jillian would've wanted.

15

JACKSON

My parents spent the rest of the weekend trying to calm me down, telling me I need to stop being angry and see a therapist. Fuck, therapy? There is nothing and no one that can fix me. Sitting and talking about my sister's death with some doctor, who has no idea what I'm going through, isn't going to help me. I don't care if it helped them.

I'm actually relieved when they finally leave after dinner. We said our goodbyes at the restaurant, and I started walking home. The problem is, I don't want to go back home. I don't want to sit alone at my place, but I also don't want to go anywhere else. I don't want to talk or feel, which leaves me aimlessly walking around town.

It's dark outside, the air crisp, and when I check the time, I realize it's almost midnight. Tucking my phone back into my pocket, I look around to see where I am. It doesn't take me long to notice I'm basically standing across the street from Kennedy's apartment complex. Fuck, can't I get away from her? Anger surges to the surface and all the calming down I've achieved by walking around evaporates into thin air. She fucking ruins everything.

Before I even think about what I'm doing, I'm across the street and walking into her apartment building. Climbing the stairs, I take them two at a time, suddenly, I have this deep, primal urge to see her, feel her like I did when she was at my place, bent over my couch with her ass in the air.

I bang my fist against her door, the sound echoes through the otherwise silent hallway.

"Open up, Kennedy," I yell at the door. "Do it, or I'll kick it down." I continue banging, not giving a shit who I wake up. I'll wake up the entire fucking building if I have to.

A moment later, the door opens, and Kennedy appears in front of me. Her silky blonde hair is in a messy bun on top of her head, and she squints her eyes at the bright light flooding into her apartment from the hallway. Clearly, I woke her up. *Oops.*

"What are you doing here?" she rasps, her voice still sleepy.

Instead of answering her, I shove past her and into her apartment without an invitation. She closes the door behind us and turns to face me, turning on a light switch beside us. At least she's starting to understand how this works. I'm tempted to bring up whatever the fuck it was that I felt on her thighs, but I want to sink my cock into her more than I care to hear what the hell is going on with her. This is all part of convincing myself that I don't care about her. If I don't ask questions, then I have nothing to care about.

"Take your clothes off. I want to fuck you again."

Her mouth falls open in shock as if she can't believe what I just said. What did she think I showed up here for in the middle of the night?

"I don't think that's a good idea."

She can't be serious, can she? Us fucking is always a good idea. It's the only good thing between us. It's either we fuck, or I'm hurting her or she's hurting me. There are no other options.

"I didn't ask you what you thought. I told you to take off your clothes." Folding my arms over my chest, I scowl down at her. "Tick tock. I don't have all night. Do it, or I do it for you."

I watch her closely as she bites her bottom lip. Nervously, she looks around the room as if she is thinking about how to get out of this.

Oh, bug, there is no getting away.

Run, and I'll just drag you back here screaming.

She doesn't look scared though, maybe uncomfortable, but not scared. Her cheeks are a light shade of pink but redden when she finally says, "In my room, lights off."

Unable to stop myself, I smirk as I give her a nod and follow her into her bedroom. The lights are off in her room, but the hallway lamp shines enough light to let me see where the bed is before she closes the door, blanketing us in darkness.

I can hear her taking her clothes off, the sound of fabric hitting the ground. I shove my shorts and boxers down in one go before tugging my shirt off over my head.

"I want you on your hands and knees. No fucking talking. I don't want to hear a whimper or cry. I just want to fuck you. You owe me that much for making me bleed the other day."

"Fine," she whispers, and I listen as she moves toward the bed, climbing up onto the mattress. Walking over to the bed, I go slow in the unfamiliar room. When I reach the bed, I feel around for her and find her as I asked, on her hands and knees.

Running a hand from her shoulder and down her arched back, I only stop when I'm cupping her firm ass. She shivers under my touch but doesn't move or say anything. Positioning myself behind her, I run both hands over her lower back and ass, enjoying how smooth her skin is. My cock is impossibly hard, and my balls ache for release.

Fuck, why do I want her so badly? I could have any girl on campus, and yet I choose the enemy.

Keeping one hand on her slender hip, I snake the other down between her legs. My fingers trace her lips, her sweet arousal coating them already. She can act like the innocent, unwilling girl all she wants, but her body doesn't lie.

She wants this, wants me to fuck her, probably as bad as I want to.

"You're wet, bug. So, fucking wet. You act like you don't want this. Like you hate me, and maybe you do, but we both know you love me fucking you." The swollen head of my cock bumps against her entrance, and I pinch her clit between my fingers. I smile at the rapid intake of air into her lungs. She grows wetter and wetter, and soon I can't help myself.

When I'm certain she's wet enough to take me, I line my cock up with her entrance and enter her in one swift shift of my hips.

Tight as a glove, she clamps down around me, and my eyes roll to the back of my head for a moment. Fuck me. Of all the girls I've fucked, no one even remotely compares to how good Kennedy feels. She shouldn't feel this good. I know it's a trap. Still, I'm willing to fall into it over and over again. Pulling all the way out, I slam into her again. I do this a couple of times, pulling myself out to the tip just to slam into her until my balls kiss her ass.

I can hear the humph sound leaving her lips with every stroke, but aside from that, she doesn't say a single word. A triumphant smile lifts my lips. I want to make her scream and chant my name from the heavens while she begs me to let her come.

As hard as it is, I go slow, keeping my strokes hard and even. Sweat drips down my back, and I grit my teeth, feeling her pussy flutter around me.

"No, you don't get to come yet," I growl, slowing once more. I take us both on this never-ending rollercoaster of almost-there pleasure. Fucking her hard and fast before coming to a stop, just to do it all over again. Kennedy is panting, but she's not begging yet.

Pistoning my hips faster, it doesn't take much to get her to the edge all over again. When I feel that she's just about to peak, I pull completely out.

"Jackson!" She sags against the mattress in defeat.

"I told you not to talk." I smack her ass hard. She whimpers, but that whimper soon becomes a moan when I slide back into her warm channel. Her slick heat tugs me deeper and deeper, and soon I'm falling into the abyss, no longer able to tease either of us anymore.

"Beg for it," I snarl as I fuck her like a savage, pressing her face into the mattress.

"Please, please..." Her sweet little voice reaches my ears, letting me know she is desperate for my cock.

"You want this cock, don't you? Want it even though you hate the person it's attached to."

"Yes, yes! Please, Jackson, please..." Squeezing her hips tighter, I slam into her to the hilt and grind my hips against her ass. Like a rocket, she goes off, her pussy clamping down on me, sending me into a spiral of pleasure.

Roaring, I can't stop myself as I erupt, filling her to the brim with my sticky seed. Falling forward, I crush her tiny body into the mattress, burying my face in her hair.

I don't want to move. I feel so sated, intensely relaxed, but I can't stay here with her. This isn't that kind of thing. I'm not about to wrap her in my arms and whisper sweet nothings in her ear.

This is all a part of the plan.

Hurting her. Breaking her.

Rolling off of her and the bed, I pull my shorts back up and tuck my cock into them. Miraculously, I somehow find my shirt in the dark and tug it back on. Slipping into my shoes, I walk to the door, lingering there for a moment, my hand hesitating over the doorknob. Why do I feel the need to ask her if she's okay? She came. I felt her pulse around me, so I know she got off. Shaking the feeling away, I open the bedroom door and leave her apartment.

Once outside, I head back to my place, feeling lighter than I have in days. Fucking Kennedy is the highlight of my day. It's almost better than taunting her or fighting with her. When I finally get to my apartment and crawl into bed, sleep evades me, and thoughts of Kennedy fill all the space in my mind.

I hate her, but part of me cares for her at the same time, and that's the problem. If only my hate for her outweighed every other emotion I felt, maybe then, I wouldn't be second-guessing myself. Maybe I wouldn't have stopped at the door, paused, and wondered if I should ask if she was okay.

She's getting under my skin, and it's time to squish those feelings because, in my heart, I know there is no room for someone so ugly.

16

KENNEDY

I hate how he uses me. How he thinks he can just show up at my apartment for a quick fuck. Even more, I hate how I let him; hate how much I enjoy it. I don't want to be that girl. Each time we've slept together, I've felt so dirty and ashamed. I'm so tired of feeling that way. I need to put an end to this before it's too late. The question is, how? I'm not stupid, there is no saying no to Jackson.

Checking the time, I realize that I'm going to be late for class if I don't start speed walking and stop daydreaming.

It's time for my creative writing class, and even though I thought about skipping again, I decided against it. I don't think I'll be able to pass if I miss anymore.

The entire way, I was praying and hoping that he wouldn't be there, but as soon as I walk in, I find him sitting in the chair behind my spot. Of course, he grins as soon as he sees me, like he's actually happy and not here to make my life a complete living hell. Taking my usual seat, I try my best to ignore him as I get out my books and papers. Even though I haven't been attending classes, Mrs. Jarrid has been sending me the assignments via email.

"How is your cunt doing? Sore?" he leans forward in his seat and whispers into my ear, his breath moving the tiny hairs against my neck. "Or are you ready for more?" When I don't answer or turn around, he continues his taunting. "I'm coming by later for more, just so you're prepared. Make sure you're nice and wet for me. You know, like normal."

Stupid. I'm so stupid, instantly my core clenches around nothing, and excitement swirls around in my belly like a tiny tornado. I hate the reaction I have to him; hate how much power he holds over my body.

"Good morning, class," Mrs. Jarrid greets everybody with a smile. "Please get out your books and turn to page two-hundred-and-forty-one."

I do as instructed and push the stupid thoughts away, preparing to do some actual learning. Reaching into my bag, I pull out a pencil and then drop the bag to the floor.

"Maybe we can fuck with the lights on this time?" Jackson whispers from behind me, and though it is a whisper, it's loud enough that the people beside us can hear every word he's saying. Ignoring him is my best bet. If I don't react, he has no ammunition.

"What, you don't want everyone to know how badly you want to ride my dick? Is that why you aren't responding? Are you ashamed?" He slashes me with another sentence, and I swear my cheeks heat to the temperature of the sun.

Why is he embarrassing both of us like this? Why can't he shut his fucking mouth? Does every little thing have to be about hurting me, breaking me down a little bit more?

Mrs. Jarrid says something up front, but I can't focus because all I can hear is Jackson panting against the back of my neck.

"You should be used to this position, facing away from me..." He doesn't get to finish his sentence because, thank you, Lord, Mrs. Jarrid interrupts him.

"Excuse me, Jackson, is there a reason you keep interrupting my class?"

"Uhh, no."

"Well, you've been warned in the past about talking when I'm talking, and since you can't seem to follow simple instructions, I'm going to have to ask you to leave."

"You're kidding, right?" Jackson huffs with disbelief, and I bite the inside of my cheek to stifle my grin. Finally, somebody puts him in his place.

"Nope, not kidding. Get out of my class, and only come back if you're going to take it seriously. I'm not a babysitter."

Jackson slams his hand down on the table, making me jump. Then I hear him shoving stuff in his bag and cursing under his breath. He's pissed. I know it without even looking at him. I watch, holding my breath as he walks out of the room, the door closing behind him.

"Now, where were we?" Mrs. Jarrid starts again, and I smile, feeling like I can finally breathe. A calmness washes over me, and I spend the rest of the class focusing on every word she says. Eventually, class comes to an end, and we're dismissed. Packing up my things slowly, I can only hope that Jackson has disappeared.

Turns out, luck isn't on my side because as soon as I walk out the door, I find him leaning against the wall, talking to another girl. She tosses her hair over her shoulder and laughs at something he says. His green eyes find mine, and I can see the fiery rage in them. He's trying to hurt me, and even though I don't want to admit it, it hurts to see him with someone else. I drop my gaze but still watch him out of the corner of my eye as he takes her hand in his, and they walk off somewhere. He doesn't hold my hand. He doesn't even look at me when we have sex.

An ugly feeling floods my veins... jealousy. I know I have no claim on Jackson. All along, I knew very well that this was nothing but sex for him. He wants nothing but revenge. He wants to hurt me in any way he can without physically touching me.

I knew all of this, and yet seeing him with another girl has my heart aching and my stomach-churning. I can handle him hating me, punishing me, even using me. But I can't handle this. I can't handle being one of his many girls, his second choice at best. The thought of him having sex with someone only hours before he has sex with me... I can't do it. Pressing a hand to my stomach, I feel the need to vomit away.

I'm such an idiot, letting my feelings get involved. Who am I kidding? My feelings were part of this all along. It's his feelings that are absent. He uses me, and I need to keep reminding myself of that.

Yes, he makes me come, and it's amazing, but that's all he'll ever give me. An orgasm and heartache. When we have sex, I forget everything around me, I forget who we are and what we are doing. For some stupid reason, I was holding on to this part of us, thinking maybe something might change. Only now do I realize how special those brief moments were to me because, for some stupid reason, I felt like they were special to him as well.

Oh, how wrong I was. Now, my eyes are open, and I know I have to end this. I have to tell him no. I just don't know how to end this without disappearing altogether.

17

JACKSON

Where the fuck is she? It's been three days, and I haven't seen her since our creative writing class. I went to her apartment, almost kicked in the door, but then decided asking the landlord to open it for me was the better choice. As I suspected, she wasn't there.

Gone, just fucking gone. Poof.

I went to each of her classes, asked the teachers, even other students... nothing. No one has seen or heard from her in three days. Three days. What if something happened to her? Someone touched her, or hurt her? Fuck. I'm going crazy just thinking about it. I tell myself I'm only worried because who will I torment if I don't have her, but I know it's deeper than that. I just don't want to acknowledge it.

Facing the fact that there is only one thing left to do. My last resort. I get out my phone and dial the number I haven't dialed in two years. I never thought I would ever call her house again. Of course, I never thought I would be fucking her either. I deleted the number the day Jillian died, but the truth is I memorized it years ago, and I'm pretty sure it will forever be etched into my mind.

For a brief second, I'm taken back in time.

"Can you please call Kennedy for me?" *Jillian yells from the Jack and Jill bathroom that we share.*

"Why can't you do it?" I groan, tugging my cell phone out of my pocket.

Jillian pops her head into my room, half of her hair is curled, and the other is stick straight. "Because unlike you, who can just show up somewhere, I have to make myself look presentable, so please, call her and ask her what time she's coming over."

"Yeah, yeah..." Not that I really have a problem with calling Kennedy. It's just thinking about her ruins my mojo for the night. I want to go on a date and not think about what my best friend, who I secretly want to bang, might be doing.

Hitting the call button on Kennedy's number, I listen as ringing fills the line, a second later, Kennedy's soft voice fills my ear.

"Hey, Jackson," she purrs, and I swear I feel the sound in my cock.

"Hey, Junebug, Jillian wants to know what time you'll be over?"

"Mmm, maybe like eight." I can see her forehead wrinkling as she thinks. God, she's so beautiful. I just need to get the balls to tell her I want more, but then there is the thing with her being both Jillian and my friend. It'll never work.

"Perfect. I'll tell her."

"Are you... are you coming tonight?" Kennedy asks with hesitation in her voice.

"Nah, I've got a date, but Ty will be there, and he said that he'll watch you guys for me."

"Oh, okay." Her voice falls flat, and it sounds like she's disappointed.

"You know you can call me if you need anything. I'll be there."

"Yeah, of course, no worries. I hope you have fun on your date." The cheer returns to her voice, and I wonder if maybe I should skip the date and hang out with them. I'd have a better time anyway.

"I will, but not as much fun as you and Jill will have tonight. Be safe, okay, bug?"

"Always."

We hang up, and something in my chest tells me to go with them, but I chalk it up to my feelings over Kennedy. I can't have her, and that's making me go a little wild.

"What did she say?" my sister yells as if she's miles away.

"Jesus, stop yelling. She said she'd be here around eight."

"*Yay!*" *She squeals, making me place my hands over my ears or risk going deaf.*

Just like that, I'm tossed from the memory and back into reality. It steals the air from my lungs and reminds me of a time when I was so carefree, and nothing could get me or keep me down. I hate it. Hate remembering a time when Kennedy was all I could ever want.

It's already late, almost ten, I might wake them up, but I don't really care. No way I'm waiting until tomorrow. Pressing the green call button, I put the phone to my ear and listen to the dial tone. A moment later, Kennedy's mom answers the phone with a cheerful *hello.*

"It's Jackson," I growl into the phone.

"Oh," is all she says.

"Is Kennedy there?" I try to keep my voice casual, but I'm pretty sure she hears how difficult this call is for me.

It takes her a few seconds to answer, my guess is she's probably as shocked about me calling as I am. *Oh, the things I fucking do for you, bug.*

"No, why would she be here?" Worry overtakes her shocked tone. Fuck, this isn't what I wanted to deal with, but without knowing where Kennedy is, that worry could be very real. "She's at Blackthorn. Isn't she?"

"No one has seen her in three days," I explain. "I thought she might have taken a trip home or something."

"Oh, my god, no." She sounds frantic at this point, and her worry is starting to spread over to me. "She hasn't been here, hasn't called either. Hold on, let me check something real quick."

I listen to the phone being set down, followed by some typing on a computer. A few moments later, she comes back on the line, her voice a little calmer now, or at least more composed.

"I just checked her credit card statement. She used her card to check into a hotel in town."

Relief washes over me, making me face the reality of how worried I was about her. "What hotel?"

"The Dunham Inn."

"I know where that is. I'll go check on her, and if there's a problem, I'll give you a call."

"Really? You would do that?"

"Yeah, I'll tell her to call you later too." I hang up the phone, grab my car keys, and head out the door.

On my way to the hotel, some of the relief I felt has already morphed back into anger. What the fuck was she thinking just taking off like that? Hiding out in some hotel? Was this her way of fighting back?

Or maybe she truly was jealous over seeing me with Crystal the other day? If I cared about her feelings, I would tell her Crystal was no one to me, that the second we rounded the corner, I pushed her away. That I even told her to leave me alone, but I'm not about to reveal that fact just to make her feel better.

Flirting with Crystal was only to hurt her feelings. I didn't really think she would be jealous and only hoped to show her that she meant nothing to me. That I could have anyone I wanted, that she wasn't anything special. Mainly, I did it to piss her off, not to run her out of school. Twenty minutes later, I pull up to the hotel and hand my keys to the valet. Walking into the lobby, I'm happy to see a young woman behind the reception counter. That's going to make all of this go so much faster.

"Hello, do you have reservations with us?" she greets.

"Hi there." I give her my most dazzling smile. "I'm actually already a guest. Unfortunately, I seem to have misplaced my key card. You wouldn't be able to make me another one, would you?" I follow up with some puppy dog eyes.

"Oh, sure, I think I could help." She giggles and bats her eyelashes at me.

"The reservations were made under Meyers."

"All I need is your ID and room number."

"Well, the problem is my wallet is in the room... and I am terrible with numbers. I checked-in three days ago. You must have not been here that day, 'cause I sure as hell would remember someone as pretty as you."

Her cheeks turn crimson red as she starts to type something on her laptop. I continue smiling, even though on the inside, I'm wishing for this to be over as soon as possible so I can get to Kennedy.

She pulls out a card and hands it to me. Giving me her best fuck me eyes, she says, "Here you go, Mr. Meyers. Room four-hundred-and-ten."

"Thanks," I snap, watching her face fall before taking the card from her finger. I spin around and head to the fourth floor. You can run my little bug, but you'll never be able to hide from me.

18

KENNEDY

*Y*ou know that strange feeling you get when you're sleeping, and you feel like someone's watching you? But there isn't any possible way that could really be happening. Not when you are locked inside a hotel room. No, that couldn't happen. Unless you have someone like Jackson in your life.

Blinking my eyes open, I've barely woken up when I let out a screech at the shadow hovering over my bed. A hand comes out of nowhere and presses against my mouth, a moment before Jackson's face comes into view. His gaze is hard, and I know instantly that I'm in trouble.

"I'm going to pull my hand away, and you're going to tell me what the fuck you're trying to prove by coming here?" The deep tone of his voice jolts my body awake, and my nipples harden against the thin material of my T-shirt, which, other than panties, is all I have on. Even with the blanket covering me, I feel so exposed and unprotected.

Pulling his hand away, he crosses his arms over his chest and stares down at me like a disappointed father.

I suck in a breath. "How the hell did you get in here?"

"Don't worry about that. Worry about answering me," he growls. He looks menacing, but I'm not scared of him.

I knew this moment would come. I knew he would find me eventually, but I didn't count on it being in the middle of the night, so I didn't prepare anything to say. What am I going to tell him? That I was jealous? He would love that. No way I'm giving him the satisfaction of knowing that. So, I say the first thing I can think of instead.

"I don't want to catch any diseases from you. If you make it a habit of sleeping around without a condom, then I'm not going to be one of your girls."

Jackson stares at me for a split second before tipping his head back and laughing. He's actually freaking laughing. A sound I haven't heard in a very long time, and if it wasn't for the situation, I might actually enjoy hearing it.

"Whatever you have to tell yourself, bug. Now be a good girl and take that shirt off. I didn't come here to talk."

Of course, he didn't. Like I would actually believe that he came here to make sure I was okay. That he was worried about me.

"I'm not having sex with you." I stand my ground, clutching onto the blanket in front of me. "Get out." I point to the door. I'm done being his whipping post. Done. I'm not doing this anymore.

"No. I didn't come all the way here just so I could turn around and go back home. I'm not leaving. At least not until I get a piece of you."

Wrinkling my nose at him, I reply, "Then get comfortable on the floor because I'm not sleeping with you."

He tilts his head to the side and raises his eyebrows like he is examining me, ready to test my limits. He's going to push me, see how far he can bend me before I snap.

"I'll tell you what. Either sex or you let me see your thighs. Which one is it going to be?"

Shaking my head furiously, strands of my blonde hair whip across my face. How did this escalate so quickly?

"No... no to both."

I know the answer between those two choices. I would rather have sex with him than let him see, but I refuse to give in. I won't let him bully me into this. He needs to leave.

"Choose, Kennedy!" he yells, his eyes piercing my soul.

"No!" Clutching the blanket to my chest, I start to scoot away from him, but I don't get far before he's on me. Grabbing the edge of the blanket, he tugs, ripping the only protection I have from him away. Like an animal that's wounded, my eyes dart around the room, looking for a place to hide. He can't see my scars, he can't. He'll use them against me, hurt me more.

I won't give him any more ammunition than he already has. I'm tired of giving him a loaded gun and expecting him not to shoot me in the heart.

With the blanket gone, I push up onto my knees and dart across the bed, but of course, Jackson anticipates the move and latches onto my ankle with his hand.

"Let me go!" I yell, my voice cracking.

He's going to find out and ruin everything. He's going to break me for the last time. Using my free leg, I kick at him, trying to get him to release my leg, but every hit reminds me of how strong he is.

"Give it up, Kennedy. Let me see what your secret is," he taunts and flips me over onto my back. Pushing up onto my elbows, I panic and lift my leg to kick him, but he tugs me to the edge of the bed, causing me to fall flat on my back again. Before I can recover, he presses his entire weight down on me. Trapping my body beneath his.

"Sex! I choose sex!" I yell out because anything is better than this.

"It's too late to choose."

"Please, Jackson, please..." I beg like I've never begged before, my heart jackhammering inside my chest. I'm barely breathing, my lungs refusing to fill with air. Any second now, he's going to find out. He's going to see the jagged scars, and everything is going to be over.

My plea reaches his ears, and a look of indifference flicks across his face, but he doesn't get up. Instead, he moves my hands into one of his own and holds them to my chest while he uses his body to hold me in place. His other hand disappears between our bodies, and then I feel it.

His fingers against my thigh. Touching the scars, tracing them.

I freeze as if I'm stuck in quicksand, and every movement sinks me deeper into the ground. Tears leak from my eyes and down my cheeks. I shiver, knowing the inevitable is going to happen. I can't stop him.

Even if it doesn't happen today, it'll happen eventually. What's the point of fighting him?

Feeling utterly defeated, I go limp in his arms. His eyebrows pinch together in confusion as he lifts his body off of mine and parts my thighs. I close my eyes and breathe through my nose, trying to defuse the panic that's claiming every cell of my body.

His breathing changes, and I cringe when I feel his gentle touch on my mutilated skin. He's inspecting them now, the rough edge of his finger traces each line.

"Who did this to you?" the words come out in a rough whisper, and I wonder if he meant to even ask the question. I don't respond, my throat too tight with fear. Everything is going to fall apart now. He knows... god, he knows.

A heartbeat passes, and another, and then I feel his hand against my cheek. His touch is gentle like a wave caressing the edge of a beach.

"Who did this to you, Kennedy? Who hurt you?" The vulnerability in his voice has my eyes flicking open without right or reason. Through my blurry vision, I look up at him. He looks like a piece of glass hanging on the edge of something. His sharp edges will cut me deeper than any self-inflicted wound if I let them.

"Kennedy. I'm trying really hard not to lose my shit, so tell me who did this to you so I can beat the fuck out of them." His jaw pops, and I know he isn't lying. He pulls away, and I shiver at the cold that rushes through me at the loss of contact.

Whiplash, that's what this is. Just five minutes ago, he was here for sex, to hurt me, and degrade me. Now he suddenly cares? Anger rushes in, flooding my mind, overtaking the panic and fear. Now I'm just furious.

"Does it matter who did it? Would you believe me if I said you did?"

"Me?" He takes a step back like I've slapped him. "I didn't fucking do that to you, and we both know it."

"You're right, you didn't physically do it. Didn't slice the skin, but you're part of the reason they're there." I pause and look away, feeling ashamed and sick that he now knows how fucked up I really am. "Why do you even care? Why does me being hurt matter to you? It's never mattered before, so don't pretend like it does now." I snap my thighs closed and scurry backward on the bed.

Jackson shakes his head and scrubs a hand down his face. "I'm not going to ask you again, Kennedy. Who did this to you? I don't give a fuck about anything else right now. Just tell me who did this to you."

I shake my head, shutting down completely.

"Tell me, or I'm calling your mother and telling her that someone is hurting you."

"ME!" I snap, "It's me. I'm hurting myself. I'm the reason there are scars on my thighs, I did it. Are you happy now? You know my secret. Go off and tell everyone. I don't care anymore." My heart cracks in my chest, and it's like every feeling I've been holding in pushes through to the surface.

"Y-you?" he chokes on the single word.

I give him a sad smile. "Yeah."

"Why would you do that? Why would you hurt yourself like that?" He isn't looking at me with disgust like I expected him to, but the look isn't necessarily pitying either. In fact, it seems like he's just seeing me for the first time. Recognizing that our pain is the same. "Why? Just tell me why so I can understand this?"

"Because... I... it just helps me deal." How am I going to explain this to him in a way he would understand when I don't really understand it? "I guess when I cut myself, everything in my mind goes silent. For one second, I don't feel guilty or ashamed." I look down at my hands, wondering what's going to happen next. Is he going to laugh in my face? Tell everyone? Now that he knows there isn't anything I can do to stop him from making me the laughing stock of the entire school.

I can't hold the tears back any longer and start to silently sob while I wait for him to mock me. My stomach twists and knots, and I feel the itch to cut myself right now to shut everything off.

"You want to do it now, don't you?" he questions.

I don't know why I bother replying, it's none of his business. I don't have to tell him what I'm thinking or feeling, but I want to. I want someone to know that I'm suffering, just one person. "I do." I sob, wiping at the tears that keep coming.

My vision is so blurry, I can't see anything, but I know he's still there.

"You can leave now. You've got what you wanted. Go tell everyone, go make a mockery out of me like I know you want to." The ache in my chest is intensifying, making it hard for me to breathe, and I gasp for air like I'm being choked.

"I'm not going anywhere. Scoot over and climb under the covers."

"Why?" I ask as I start doing as he says. I'm so used to doing what he tells me, I simply act and ask questions later.

"Because I want to hold you, that's why. Now don't ruin this. Roll over and let me do this."

"I don't want your pity."

"I don't pity you, Kennedy. In fact, for the first time in forever, I think we actually might have something in common. Now roll over before I make you."

Doing as he says, I roll over and pull the blanket up to my chest. A moment later, I hear clothes hitting the floor, and then he's crawling under the blanket and moving toward me. Heat envelopes my body, and when he puts his arm over me and tugs me back into his bare chest, I feel... safe, which is the strangest thing since he's the last person I should feel safe with.

"What do you mean by we have something in common?"

"I feel the same about fighting in the pit. I like kicking the shit out of someone, but I don't mind getting my face smashed in either. Physical pain is better than the alternative, isn't it?"

"Yeah..."

"Sleep. Your secret is safe with me, Junebug." He uses the nickname he used to call me when we were younger, and my heart shatters. I sob into the pillow while he holds me tight, holding all my broken pieces together. Then, I close my eyes and fall into a fitful sleep, wondering if he really means it.

Is my secret safe with him?

19

JACKSON

Seeing her pain for the first time is like ripping the scab off an already healing wound. I thought what I was doing was the right thing. I thought she was bluffing, pretending that she felt bad, but the proof was right there. I thought that discovering her pain—seeing her suffer—would give me more satisfaction than it did. Instead, it made me sick, made me hate myself a little bit. Knowing she was cutting herself, causing herself physical pain. All along, she had been suffering right in front of me. I was just too self-absorbed to see it. Too wrapped up in my own pain, in wanting to make sure she was hurting, to notice that she was.

I spent all night holding her in my arms, listening to her sob. I can't wrap my head around her thinking I was going to tell. Make fun of her. I almost scoff at the thought. It's totally understandable why she would think that, but I'm not that big of an asshole. I won't have her doing it anymore now that I know though.

What if she cuts herself too deep?

I can't have her death on my conscience, and I can't lose her. I don't know if I'm ready to forgive her or if I ever fully can, but I don't want to lose her.

After not sleeping a lick, I drove back to my apartment just as the sun was rising. Yes, I'm a pussy. I didn't want to be there when she woke up. Mainly because I'm not sure what I should say to her. I don't know how to react to the knowledge that she's been hurting herself, cutting herself for god knows how long to deal with the pain.

I think about what my mother told me as I toss a ball at the wall and catch it. I haven't dealt with my sister's death because I feel like the moment that I do, the moment that I accept she's dead, I'll start the process of moving on, of forgetting her, and I can't imagine ever forgetting someone like her, even if she is dead.

Then the shit with Kennedy makes me feel guilty, it makes me feel like I'm betraying my sister. Yet, I can't shut off the fact that I care about her.

Sighing into the empty room, I wonder what Jillian would want me to do? Would she approve of me caring for Kennedy? Would she be okay with me forgiving her?

Confusion seeps into my bones. I don't get a chance to focus on it, though, because my cell phone starts ringing, interrupting my thought process. I grab the device from beside me and look at the screen.

It's my mother. I haven't talked to her in some time, and I kinda miss her. Hitting the green answer key, I put the phone on speaker.

"Hey, Mom."

"Hi, sweetheart, how are you?"

"I'm doing good."

"You don't sound good, you sound sad. Is everything okay?" Of course, my mom can read me, even over the phone. Must be some motherly instinct or some shit.

"I'm sorry about acting like a total ass last weekend. Kennedy ran off because of it. Like left school and hid out in a hotel." I mean, that's not the complete reason, but I'm not telling her everything. Some things my mother doesn't need to know.

"Oh, Jackson, I know you're still hurting, but it wasn't Kennedy's fault. It was an accident. Yes, Kennedy made a stupid choice, but she was so young, and people make a lot of mistakes when they are young. I know in my heart, she would never hurt anyone on purpose, least of all her best friend. She loved Jillian, probably as much as you did."

Damnit. There isn't any denying what she says. Jillian and

Kennedy were connected at the hip. They loved each other as much as any sisters could. I know it because I was afraid that if I ever made a move on Kennedy, it might ruin her relationship with my sister, and I couldn't risk that.

"I know, but it's so hard to let that go. It's so hard not to blame her when if she had just waited for me, things might have been different."

"You're right, things might've been different, or they might not. Your sister could've got in a car accident later on, anything could've happened. It's important to remember that tomorrow is never promised. Your sister's death opened our eyes to that, and I wish it would open your eyes too." I kinda sorta hate how right she sounds right now.

"I just... I feel like if I let it go, if I start to forgive, to move on..." my throat tightens, "I feel like I'll forget her. If I don't remind myself every day, then I'll forget her..."

"You'll never forget her. She's your twin, a piece of her lives inside of you, and we both know she would be angry as hell to see you and Kennedy suffering because of her." A smile tugs at my lips as I picture my sister staring me down, her hands on her hips. "I promise, it's the only way to move forward. It's time for you to start living your life without carrying around all that pain, all of the time. It doesn't have to be this way, Jackson."

She's right, she's so right, but I'm not sure if I can forgive and forget so easily. It still feels like she died yesterday. I can start to try though.

"Okay, I'll try, Mom."

"That sounds wonderful, sweetheart." I can see her smile in my mind, and I know she is happy about this. Happy that I'm taking the first steps of learning how to deal with Jillian's death. "Why don't you come home to visit next month?"

"Sure, why not. I'll look at some dates and call you in a few days."

"Great!"

"One more question... did you get Kennedy's cell number while you were here?"

"Yes, why?"

"Can you send it to me? I want to talk to her."

"Sure, I'll send it right over. Please, be kind to her, Son. She blames herself enough, and even though you don't want to believe it, she lost Jillian too."

"I know, Mom."

We say our I love yous and then hang up. Part of me feels the phone call was what I needed. I'm terrified of what will happen next, but this has to happen eventually. Being angry and bitter every day is killing me on the inside. Destroying the best parts of me. Jillian would kill me if she was here right now and saw the way I've been acting.

My thoughts of Kennedy swirl, and I wonder how I'm going to approach this with her. She's my trigger in the big mess of things. Scrolling through my phone, I open my mom's text and save Kennedy's contact info. I'm tempted to go over to her place, but then I'll want to fuck her, and I won't get to say what I want. Plus, I'm not sure she is ready for sex yet, and I don't want to push it. I'm going to do my best not to hurt her anymore. I don't want to be the reason she continues to hurt herself.

So, I send her a text that says, *hey.*

Instantly, I get a reply.

K: Who is this?

I contemplate telling her that it's Jackson, but I figure what I'm about to say is enough knowledge for her to get the hint.

Me: You can't cut yourself anymore. If you do, I'm telling someone. I won't let you hurt yourself anymore. Promise me you won't.

I hit send before I can stop myself. I'm reaching that point where I want to just shut down and say fuck it, but this is part of moving on, and I can only deny that I care about her for so long. It's time to face the music.

K: Promise.

Reading her single word text, I don't trust that she really means it, so I send her another.

Me: On Jillian's grave.

My phone dings, and I imagine she's staring at her screen with the same conviction I am.

K: On Jillian's grave.

Dropping the phone onto the mattress, I tip my head back into the pillows and let my mind wander. Maybe I can forgive Kennedy? Maybe I can let go of the pain? Or maybe I can't? At the very least, I know Kennedy won't be hurting herself anymore, and that's the most important thing of all because if she ever killed herself because of me, I wouldn't forgive myself. It'd be like losing Jillian all over again, and I doubt I could survive that.

20

KENNEDY

Life seems to be headed in the right direction. For once, I feel like I'm not suffocating. Like I'm swimming back to the surface, instead of being dragged down deeper. The fact that Jackson isn't doing everything in his power to make my life hell helps immensely.

We've come to this strange agreement that we aren't quite friends, but we aren't enemies either. Every day I see a little bit of the old Jackson returning. He smiles more, laughs, and seems as if he too is healing.

I still wait with bated breath for the other shoe to drop. How long is he going to keep up this act of caring before he snaps on me again? I keep hoping things will stay this way, and we can heal together, but I'm not stupid enough to believe that'll happen.

As sad as it is, I'm wary of every little thing he does. I don't understand how he flipped a switch, how he went from hating me so passionately to showing he cares in the blink of an eye. It's not like he goes out of his way for me, but he also doesn't actively try to make my life difficult anymore.

Descending the steps outside of my economics class, I find Jackson sitting casually against a bench. He looks ruggedly handsome in nothing more than jeans and a T-shirt. He's surrounded by his friends, or at least, I assume they're his friends. I stare at him for a second longer than necessary before turning to walk toward my apartment.

I'm not a part of his life in that way, and I'm okay with that. I'm okay with being alone because I'm used to it. I can't say I don't miss being his best friend, hearing his laugh, and watching him smile. His joy was once my joy. I used to think I loved him, and part of me still feels that way. I don't think you can stop loving someone once you've started. Your love for them just changes.

Halfway home, I get this odd feeling that someone is following me. Shivering, I turn around to look over my shoulder and find that Jackson is behind me. I'm not sure if him being here is a good or a bad thing yet, but I'll slow down anyway so he can catch up with me.

"Hey," he greets, his hands shoved in his pockets.

"Hey," I reply as he falls into step next to me.

In an awkward silence, we walk side by side the entire way home. When we get to my apartment complex, I wonder what his next move is? Is he going to leave? Come in? He answers my questions without even knowing it when he continues walking with me up to my door.

"I'm coming inside," he tells me. I guess we're still not on asking terms. "I want to check your thighs. Make sure you've kept your promise."

"I did."

"Then you won't mind showing me, right?"

"Right," I huff.

He follows me up the stairs and into my apartment. I drop my backpack on the ground and take off my sweater jacket while Jackson closes the door behind us, locking the deadbolt into place. Leaning against the door, he crosses his arms in front of his chest and looks down at my jeans, motioning for me to take them off. He doesn't seem annoyed or even impatient, so I should be thankful for that. I know he's already seen my scars, but the thought of showing him them again is frightening all the same.

"Show me," he orders, pushing off the door, taking a step closer.

Insecurity takes hold of me as I start to unbutton my jeans with shaky hands. Careful not to drag my panties down too, I shimmy my jeans down my legs, exposing my thighs to him.

He closes the distance between us and gets down on one knee to inspect the scarred area even further. I close my eyes, unable to look at his face while he does this. I don't want to see the disgust or pity in his eyes. I shiver at the contact, wondering what he's thinking?

Hot breath fans against my thigh, a moment before lips brush over my skin. His lips against my skin is like a firework going off in an enclosed space. My eyes fly wide open, and I stare down at him, watching as he places soft kisses over the uneven skin.

"What are you doing?" I ask, a light tremble in my voice. I'm ready to push him away, shove his body away from mine, even though part of me wants to pull him closer.

He places one last kiss on my leg, peering up at me while he does before pushing himself off the floor to a stand.

I open my mouth to speak, but before a single syllable can make it out, his lips are on mine. My eyes flutter closed on instinct, and I give in to the feeling... give in to him.

I don't want to need him, but I know a part of me does. I've come to love these secret moments we share together, where we're not Jackson or Kennedy but two entirely different people. His arms wrap around me, and like putty in his hands, I mold to him, my body curving into his. His tongue darts out and runs over my bottom lip, begging for entry, and I part my lips, granting him access.

He tastes like fresh mint and sin, wrapped all in one. I can't stifle the groan that slips from my throat, but that doesn't matter because Jackson swallows the noise, his tongue gliding against mine with ease.

This isn't my first kiss, but it almost feels like it is. Because nothing I've ever done has felt the way this kiss feels. All-consuming, provoking, searing. It's one of those kisses you won't forget, that will be forever ingrained in your mind.

One of his hands stays on my lower back while the other travels down over my butt. He strokes me there before giving it a tight squeeze.

Only then do I remember that I'm standing here with my pants down to my ankles.

Jackson doesn't seem to mind, judging by his hardness, which is pressing into my lower belly. His other hand moves lower until both are cupping my ass.

Without ever breaking the kiss, he picks me up and carries me into the bedroom. Snaking my arms around his neck, I hold onto him like he is my lifeline.

Once in the room, he gently places me on the mattress, breaking our kiss. Opening my eyes, I find he's hovering above me, his lips swollen from our kiss. There is something different about this moment. Every time we've ever had sex, it was me facing away from him, and we never kissed, not once.

"I need you," he whispers, and I understand what he's trying to ask.

"I need you too," I confess.

It doesn't take him but a second to strip out of his clothing. He is completely naked, but my eyes are glued to his chest as he takes my shoes off and throws them next to the bed. Then he pulls my pants down the rest of the way, followed by my panties. My shirt is next. Once that's gone, he reaches behind me to unclasp my bra so I can slide it off.

Even though we've had sex twice, we've never seen each other fully naked. I feel like we are just now discovering each other, seeing one another for the first time. I let my gaze wander over every inch of his body, his muscled chest that leads down to sculpted abs, and the deep V in his groin. My mouth waters, and I reach for him, wanting to touch, trace each line. I want to memorize it all, to hold onto this moment permanently.

I don't know if this is a one-time thing or something more.

Right now, though, I'll pretend it's forever. That he is my forever.

Leaning down, he lowers his head and takes one of my hardened nipples into his wet, warm, mouth. Pleasure zings through my body, and I bury my fingers into his thick dark hair. As he sucks harder, I use my hand to hold his head in place, not wanting him to stop.

He chuckles against my skin but doesn't stop swirling his tongue around the hard nub. Pleasure blooms deep in my core, and I lift my hips, beckoning him to the area I want.

When he pulls away, I think I might be getting my wish, but he only moves to the other side, giving the nipple there equal attention. While his mouth is busy with my breasts, his hands are busy tracing each and every contour of my body. It's like he's mapping out my body, trying to etch an image into his mind just like I am.

Before, he was using my body for his own pleasure, and today, he is worshipping it, giving me pleasure like I've never felt before. Caring for me, showing me a different side of him altogether.

"I don't want to go too fast, but I really want to be inside you." He pulls away and sighs against my skin as he presses open-mouthed kisses against my stomach, moving lower with each one. I'm drowning in him, his scent, his touch, the way his lips caress my skin. He's owning another sliver of my heart, and I don't even think he knows it.

"Yes, fuck me," I say, letting my need for him drip into my words.

"I will just let me make sure you're ready." The deep baritone of his voice makes me shiver, and when I feel his hand moving between my legs, I part my thighs, seeking out his touch. His fingers trace over my folds, gently flicking my clit in the process.

I'm so needy that I gasp and arch upward into his hand. A flush creeps up my chest and over my face, and I feel so hot, I think I might be melting.

"So fucking responsive, you have no idea how beautiful you are, how long I've wanted this. I told myself that hate was all I felt for you, but I knew I was lying from the start. Hating you has always been easy, but admitting that I want you is something else entirely."

Licking my lips, I open my mouth to reply, but the words get lost somewhere in my throat when Jackson slowly enters me with two thick digits.

Everything else fades away for a brief moment as he fucks me with his fingers, slow and deep, bringing me to the brink of pleasure before easing out of me. I want to tell him to put his fingers back inside of me, but he crawls up over my body and hooks one of my legs over his hip, nestling himself between my thighs.

Dragging his cock through my arousal, I let out a sigh, clawing at his chest, needing him closer.

"Soon, Junebug, I know you're eager, but I want to drag this out as long as I can."

A deep groan rumbles out of his chest as I sink my nails into his skin and bite at his bottom lip, urging him to get on with it.

The mushroom head of his cock grazes my entrance, and I lift my hips just a smidge, and like magic, he sinks deep inside of me. That one single stroke makes my stomach quake, and I shiver at the intensity of pleasure that ripples through me.

"Fuck. I never think it can get better, but every time it does."

"Sooo good," I whimper, holding onto his biceps as he slowly moves his hips, each deep penetrating stroke driving me closer to the heavens.

Jackson grits his teeth and continues his punishingly slow pace, making love to me, and piecing all the broken pieces of my heart back together. With him, I feel everything, all the emotions I want to escape, he makes me feel each one when he's inside of me.

Moving faster, he buries his face in the crook of my neck. Using one arm to hold himself up and the other to keep my leg in place against his hip, he drives into me, over and over again, until I'm consumed by him. Until there is nothing left in the world besides him and me.

There is no escaping the orgasm that lays claim to me right then, zinging up my spine, making me feel completely weightless. My pussy flutters around his length, and Jackson hisses into my skin as he continues to move through my peak. A few more strokes and he too meets his release, his warm release filling me to the brim, and trickling out onto my thighs.

I'm on cloud nine, and nowhere near coming down. The weight of Jackson's body on mine makes me feel secure and protected. I want to stay like this forever but know all too well, that soon he'll pull away, tug on his clothes, and disappear into the night.

Maybe this time it'll be different?

Rolling off of me, he lies back against the mattress, his chest heaving, matching the rise and fall of my own. I'm not sure what to do, so I just lie there, waiting to see what happens next. After a while, he gets out of bed and like I suspected, starts putting his clothes on. Grabbing the comforter from the edge of the bed, I drag it up to my chest, covering myself.

I can feel Jackson's eyes on me, but I can't look at him. I don't know why I thought this would be different. Why had I even hoped? I'm stupid. We may not be enemies, but we certainly aren't anything else.

"This is nice... I mean, sex with you is great, fantastic even, but that's all it can ever be."

"I know," I whisper, leaning back against the headboard. I can still feel his release against my thighs.

"Good. Maybe we're not enemies anymore, but we aren't friends either. I don't know what the hell we are or even what we're doing, but it can't ever be more than sex, Kennedy. Okay?" It's like he's reassuring himself more than me, but I don't say that. I don't want to fight with him after sharing such an incredible moment together.

"I understand," I tell him, hiding the emotions from my voice. I lift my gaze up and away from my hands and find him staring at me. I can't make out what he's thinking, but I'm not really trying either. All I'll ever be to him is someone to get off with. Someone he can use for pleasure and discard afterward.

Nothing more, nothing less.

Without saying goodbye, he walks out of my apartment. The pieces of my heart that I was sure he'd fused back together, shatter all over again. I roll over and sob into the pillow that smells like us, wishing that things could be different because, for once, I truly don't want to feel like I deserve to be reminded of the past. I want to heal and move on.

I just don't think it'll be with Jackson.

21

JACKSON

When Talon asked me to come with him, I thought going to a party was what I needed. I've spent the last few days staying out of Kennedy's way. After the sex we had the other night, I figured I needed a breather. I'm on the verge of getting too attached to her, too intimate. Something that can't happen. I'm just figuring out how not to hate her. I can't deal with any other feeling growing.

So, my solution... coming to this party. Turns out, I was wrong. There isn't shit here for me. I sit on a couch in the frat house, a cup of cold beer in my hand. My friends are laughing and talking. Chicks are running around rampant with little to no clothing on just begging to be fucked, and I can't seem to think about anything but Kennedy.

What's she doing right now?

She has been on my mind constantly. Even when I don't intend to think about her, I do. I worry about her, wonder how she's coping, but I can't bring myself to ask. It's like the only way I know how to communicate with her is through the use of my body.

A hand lands on my shoulder, and I turn to look down at it.

"Jackson," Crystal purrs into my ear a moment later. I'm tempted to shrug her hand off. "Are you ignoring me?" She twists her body, so her tits are brushing against my arm.

"Nope, not ignoring you. Didn't even know you were here." I try not to sound like a dick, but she'd know if I was interested, which I'm not.

"Well, now, you know." She giggles, and it's like nails on a chalkboard. I'm so annoyed, I tighten my grasp on the cup in my hand.

"Yup," I grind out.

Talon is watching me out of the corner of his eye, probably waiting for me to explode.

"Do you want to go upstairs with me?" She leans in closer, rubbing her tits on me like a cat in heat. Her teeth graze my ear, and I've had enough. This feels wrong, all fucking wrong. I jump up off the couch, sloshing some of the beer out of my cup in the process.

I can feel everyone in our small circle gawking at me, and I need to get the fuck out of here. This isn't where I want to be, and these aren't the people I want to be with right now.

"I'm leaving, man," I tell Talon, who has some chick sitting on his lap. She's grinding her ass against his groin so I wouldn't be surprised if he didn't hear me.

"You sure?" he asks, surprising me.

"Yeah, are you sure you want to leave so soon?" Crystal pouts, leaning against the couch, giving me a full view of her cleavage, which is bursting from her V-neck shirt. All I can do is shake my head.

"I'm not interested," I growl.

Turning away from them, I don't say anything else and walk out of the room. On the way out, I toss my half drank beer onto the lawn, right along with the cup. Pulling my phone out of my pocket, I check the time, wondering if Kennedy is still awake. I could call her, but what would be the fun in that?

Taking the chance that she is, I get in my car and drive over to her place. I find a parking spot and then walk inside. By the time I reach her door, I'm only second-guessing myself a little bit about coming here. I'm still angry, and I'll always be sad, but like my mother told me, she lost Jillian that night too. Maybe we can be sad and angry together for a while?

Knocking on her door, I wait impatiently to see her beautiful face. I never thought I would be able to look at her, see her scar, without seeing Jillian dead, but the pain has eased each day since I decided to stop holding onto it.

Time ticks by slowly, and I tug my phone out to call her just as the lock disengages, and the door clicks open.

"Oh, hey," Kennedy gives me a tight-lipped smile.

She looks tired, and for a second, I consider asking her if she's sleeping at night. Am I ready to insert myself more into her life? To show I care?

"Is everything okay?" she asks when I don't say anything.

"Uh, yeah. I was just wondering if you wanted to go out for a late dinner or something?"

Her eyes go wide with shock and her pink lips purse together. I'm tempted to kiss and nibble on them, but for now, I'm content just watching her lips move as she talks.

"Are you sure?" she asks, tucking a strand of her blonde hair behind her ear.

"No, not really. This might be a terrible idea," I tell her honestly. "I was just at a party, but I kind of got tired of the people there, so I left and came here."

"I don't know about going out," she says as she shifts her legs nervously. "I'd rather stay in and eat or watch a movie or something."

If she was any other girl, I'd think she was trying to get me to have sex with her. But knowing how she is, I truly believe her. Since she's been here at Blackthorn, she hasn't been anywhere apart from campus, her apartment, and the one-time trip to the pits. She doesn't go out to eat, to movies, or parties. Hell, she doesn't even like to ride in the car.

"Would you be okay riding in the car with me to my place? We can pick up some takeout on the way." Again, shock colors her features, she visibly pales, and I'm starting to wonder if it's because she is anxious about going out or if she is actually scared to come with me. After a moment, she eases my mind by nodding her head.

"Sure, I'll ride in the car with you. Let me put my shoes on and get my jacket." She disappears from my view for a few moments and reappears dressed and ready. She locks the door behind her, and we walk down the stairs together.

When we get to my car, I can see how nervous she is. Was she this nervous last time? I think I was too riled up to pay attention then. Again, I'm taken aback by how much the accident continues to affect her and how much I ignored the signs before.

"You sure you're okay?"

"Yeah, I need to stop avoiding this. I can't expect my parents to drive me around for the rest of my life, plus, never going anywhere in a car is unrealistic." She opens the door on her side and slides into the passenger seat while I get into the driver's seat.

"I didn't know it bothered you that much to ride in cars. Have you driven since..." I can't even say it out loud.

"No, and I won't. I'm not ready. I tried once and had the biggest panic attack of my life. I'd rather walk everywhere. It's really not that bad... walking, I mean. Exercise, you know."

I nod, knowing that she is just trying to reason with her idea of walking everywhere. I turn on the car and watch her out of the corner of my eye as she quickly straps her seatbelt in place.

"I'll drive slow," I assure her as I pull out of the parking spot.

Her body is rigged as I drive, only relaxing a little when we make a quick stop at the drive-through fast food place. I order for both of us, surprising myself by remembering what she likes. When I look over to confirm I got it right, she gives me a little smile and nods her head.

I pay for both of us, and the lady hands us two bags of food through the window. As I pull back out of the parking lot, I hear a deep rumbling noise.

"Was that your stomach growling?"

"I guess I didn't realize how hungry I was until I smelled this deliciousness." Kennedy's giggles fill the car. A sound I haven't heard in a very long time. Listening to Crystal's giggle earlier made me cringe, but hearing Kennedy do it makes me smile.

"Jesus, start eating some French fries before your stomach makes that sound again, and I go deaf." Her giggles turn into a full-on laugh, and I can't help but laugh with her.

"Fine, I'll eat some on the way, since you're making me." She opens the bag and starts picking out fries one by one, nibbling on them in an adorable way.

"Let me have some," I say and open my mouth. She grabs a few and starts feeding me while I keep my eyes on the road and my hands on the steering wheel. The rest of the way to my place, she alternates between eating a fry and feeding me one. By the time I pull up to my building, the bag must be half empty. I kill the engine, and we get out of the car.

Walking up to the apartment, I don't miss how normal this feels. Her coming over to my place, eating dinner, and hanging out. Almost like we used to do.

The rest of the dinner feels just as natural. We get comfortable on the couch while eating our burgers and the leftover fries. I turn on *Modern Family* since it's light and funny. We eat, talk, and laugh. I don't recall when I last felt this content. It's not quite happiness yet, but it's a far cry from the misery I was stuck in for the last two years.

After the sixth episode, I notice how Kennedy has gotten increasingly quiet, and her head starts to lull to the side. I contemplate taking her back home, or telling her to go to my bed, but before I can make up my mind, her body slumps against me and her cheek is flat against my arm.

I look down at her cuddled up to my side. Her lips are slightly parted, and a soft moan escapes them. That little sound, combined with her body pressed up against mine, has my cock hard in two seconds.

Shifting, I try to move us to get more comfortable, but the motion just wakes her up. Immediately, her eyes go wide, realizing what had happened.

"I'm sorry, I didn't mean to fall asleep," she says, pulling away. "I should probably go home." She starts to get up from the couch, but I grab her wrist and pull her back.

"It's okay. I was just trying to get comfortable. And it's late, you can stay here." I pause, trying to figure out the sleeping arrangements.

Maybe I should sleep on the couch? No, not happening. "Come on, let's go to bed."

"Okay," she agrees, but I don't miss the reluctance in her voice. She isn't sure about this. *Well, that makes two of us.*

Leading her into the bedroom, I start stripping out of my clothes while watching her do the same. Before she gets to her bra, I grab a shirt from my dresser and hand it to her. She makes quick work of her bra before slipping on the way-too-big shirt. As I'm standing there, staring at her, I realize she's the first girl to ever step foot in my room, to ever be given the option of sleeping in my bed.

When I fuck chicks, it's usually quick, and never anything tender, or intimate. This is intimate, and I don't know how I feel about it yet. My gaze drops down to her creamy white thighs, scars or not, they make my mouth water. I haven't eaten her out yet. I wanted to the other night but got sidetracked by her tits.

Laughing internally at myself, I must let a grin slip because Kennedy is looking at me funny. "What?"

"You're just smiling, and it's weird because you don't normally do that."

"Do too, just not often."

She walks over to the side of the bed and tugs back the sheets before settling onto the mattress. It annoys me how perfect she looks there—like she was always meant to be in my bed. Guilt bleeds into my subconscious, and I push it away. Nostrils flaring, I breathe through my nose and get nothing but a whiff of her feminine scent.

"You okay? I can go home, really it's not a big deal."

"No, just... come here." I pat the spot in front of me on the bed. "Lie on your back and spread your legs."

"W-why?" Kennedy stutters as if she's nervous but does as I ask.

Situated on her back in front of me, her legs spread wide and her eyes peering up at me with curiosity, I feel as if she's truly at my mercy. She looks as if she's comfortable in my presence and not so rigid. Like I could do anything I wanted to her, and she would allow it.

"I want to taste you," I croak, giving away the effect she has on me.

She doesn't object, so I reach for the hem of the shirt and push it up. Kennedy is unlike all the other girls I've done things with. She is simple, but absolutely perfect at the same time, and I didn't realize how much I needed that in my life until now. Dipping my fingers into the sides of her panties, she lifts her butt and helps me so I can drag them down her legs.

Tossing the panties over my shoulder, I drop down to my knees while spreading her thighs wider with my hands. My gaze catches on her scars, reminding me of how fragile she is, of how we're both suffering.

Stop. Don't think about that right now.

Directing my gaze back to her pink pussy, I lean in and run my nose up and down between her folds. A soft gasp fills the room, and I smile, giving her little clit a flick of my tongue. Eating pussy was never high on my to-do list with others, but like all the other things, Kennedy is the exception. I don't feel obligated to do this. I want to, need to.

Gripping onto her thighs a little tighter, I bend her legs back toward her chest, giving myself a better view. Then I start feasting. I devour every inch of her, licking, nibbling, and sucking on her perfect pussy.

Moving down to her entrance, I circle it with my tongue before dipping inside, fucking her with shallow strokes.

"Jackson," she gasps, and her legs start to shake, but I don't stop. Pressing a thumb to her clit, I rub gentle circles against it and tongue fuck her, enjoying every drop of arousal that coats my tongue. "I'm... oh, god..." She whimpers, pulling me closer, before trying to push me away.

Chuckling into her pussy, the sound rumbles through her, encouraging her release further.

"I... It feels so good..." Another whimper of pleasure falls from her lips, and it's pure pleasure to my ears.

Helplessly, she tries to wiggle away from me, to close her legs, but I hold her in place until she finally explodes, her release coating my lips and dribbling down my chin.

Then I suck and lick her until I've cleaned every drop from her swollen pussy. Releasing her, I almost laugh at how sedated she looks. My cock is rock hard and ready to feel her lips wrapped around it, but when I reach for the waistband of my boxers, I notice Kennedy clamping up.

"I... you shouldn't have done that. I won't... I can't return the favor."

"What do you mean you can't return the favor? You've never given a blow job before?" I mean, I wouldn't be surprised, she was a virgin, after all. Maybe she hasn't, and that's why she's nervous.

Then I remember how she freaked out the first time I tried to get her to blow me. Guilt gnaws on me at the thought of how I treated her then.

Her eyes skirt away from mine, and fear trickles into her features. "I...just don't like it. It makes me sick." The lie rolls off of her tongue, and I'm a little angry that she's not telling me the truth about this. If she doesn't want to do it, she can say that. There isn't any need to lie about it.

I'm half tempted to push the subject but don't want to ruin the night that we've had. This is progress even if it's small.

"It's fine, get under the covers so we can go to bed," I say. My cock is cursing me out right now, and my balls will probably be blue by the morning, but it is what it is.

Kennedy doesn't object and is under the covers in seconds. I crawl in as well and shut off the light. Rolling over, I toss an arm over her slender body and tug her back toward me. She curls into my side like a kitten, like she was made to be there.

It takes a bit for sleep to find me, but once it does, I find it's the best night's sleep I've had in months, and I wonder if it has anything to do with the blonde-haired girl sleeping beside me.

22

KENNEDY

*E*ating lunch in the cafeteria is my least favorite thing ever, but I'm dragging today after getting up early to leave Jackson's apartment and walk home. Placing a salad and water on my tray, I pay for my stuff and head to one of the tables away from everyone else.

I've just pierced a piece of lettuce with my fork and am bringing it to my lips when a cackling group of girls comes walking in. I keep my eyes trained on my food and do my best to ignore them. Crystal is leading the pack, while I don't know her personally, I saw her that one time with Jackson in the hallway, but I've also heard about her. She's considered popular here at Blackthorn.

Out of the corner of my eye, I watch them get their food.

When they start walking toward my table, I consider getting up to toss my food out, but why should I have to leave. I was here first.

As if she can sense my disdain, she walks around the table and takes a seat two spots away from me. Trays slam against the table, and I stab my food like it's a living object that I'm trying to kill.

"Oh, my god, guys, last night was amazing," Crystal exclaims.

"Yeah? Heard you were with Jackson? Are you guys like a thing now?" One of her friends asks.

I nearly roll my eyes, a thing?

"Not officially, but I'm pretty sure he wants to be. After spending the entire time at the party with me, he left and then called me this morning to come over." The hold I have on my fork tightens, the metal digging into my skin. I don't want to admit the way I'm feeling right now. I don't want to think about it, but I can't escape it, not when it's right in front of me.

Jackson's words from last night ring in my ear. *"I was just at a party, but I kind of got tired of the people there, so I left and came here."*

Was he really there with her hours before he was with me? And did he really call her over after I left his place? This morning? He probably did because, unlike me, she doesn't have a problem sucking his dick. Tears prick at my eyes. Part of me doesn't want to believe that. What we did last night was special. There is no way I imagined it all. But the insecure part of me, the fragile part of me, does believe her. He's tried to hurt me before.

Could last night have been a game to him? A new way to hurt me? Is he building me up just to break me down again? I look down at the salad, my appetite shrinking. I can't stomach sitting here any longer, listening to something that may or may not be true.

Just as I go to place my fork down on the tray, I look up and spot Jackson and his friend, Talon, walking into the cafeteria. Oh, great, now everyone can laugh at me together. Once they're closer, Crystal starts to squirm in her seat as if she's a little kid who has to pee.

"Jackson," Crystal purrs, as they approach the table, and acid bubbles up in my throat. "I'm so glad you're here."

I think I'm going to be sick.

"Yeah, I bet," Jackson replies but doesn't even look in her direction.

In fact, his eyes are on me, burning through my clothes and into my skin. I feel as if I'm under a microscope being inspected.

"Come sit with us. There's plenty of room." Crystal pats the seat next to her, and I wonder if she can see how desperate she is being in that moment. Then again, I don't know why I care how desperate she acts. I'm not in competition with her. Jackson and I aren't even friends, let alone anything past that.

"Nah, I'm going to sit with Kennedy," Jackson says, shocking the hell out of me as he takes the seat in front of me. Talon follows suit, taking the spot beside him.

"Hey," Talon greets me, and my cheeks burn with fire.

"Hey," I whisper back.

"Talon, Kennedy. Kennedy, Talon," Jackson introduces us, and it seems like everyone in the room is staring at me. I'm not sure what to say. It's not like these people are my friends.

I can see Crystal out of the corner of my eye. She looks like she's ready to scratch my eyes out, little does she know there isn't anything going on between us.

"Jackson, you know, I was thinking, maybe we could hang out again, we have so much fun every time we're together." Her teeth sink into her bottom lip, and she bats her eyes at him, and I grab my tray, preparing to leave, but stop when I see that Jackson isn't even looking at her. He's watching me. He hasn't looked her way once, and in fact, from the tightness in his jaw and tension in his eyes, I could only guess that he's annoyed.

A second passes, and then another, no one says anything, and like a hurricane making landfall, Crystal explodes.

"You don't have to ignore me, especially not for some geek with an ugly ass scar on her face." Crystal and her friends break out in laughter as her words slice through me. I try and cover up my shock with a mask of indifference before Jackson can see it, but it's too late. Fury overtakes his features, and I'm half tempted to tell him he doesn't have to stick up for me, but keep my mouth shut.

"I'm not ignoring you because of Kennedy. I'm ignoring you because you're clingy and annoying, and I'm not interested. I've said it ten times. How much clearer do you need it to be?" Crystal's face looks as if she's tasted something sour.

"Excuse me, but no one says no to me. Every guy wants me, even you. You just won't admit it." She purses her lips. "Isn't that right, even you want me, Talon?"

Talon shrugs. "I mean, I'd fuck you, but you aren't the type I'd keep around."

Crystal and all her friends gasp in shock, and I decide to make my exit. I don't want to be a part of this squabble any longer. I'm not anything to Jackson, and I don't want him to feel obligated to stick up for me anymore.

Grabbing my tray, I get up from my seat and walk to the trash. Dumping the half-eaten salad into the garbage, I do my best not to run out of the cafeteria. I make it through the double doors and down a set of steps before I hear someone running behind me. Glancing over my shoulder, I find Jackson running toward me.

"What the hell, Kennedy?" he growls as he reaches me, his breathing harsh.

"I..." What do I even say?

"You didn't have to leave because of her. She would've left all on her own."

I tuck a stray strand of hair behind my ear and look up at him. "You didn't have to stick up for me, and I wasn't going to stay there and watch a fight ensue that I had no right being a part of. Those are your friends. Plus, I was done eating, anyway."

Jackson's brows furrow, and his nostrils flare. "You still had a whole salad, and you didn't even open your water."

I shrug, knowing I've been caught in a lie. "I lost my appetite. Anyway, I'm fine. Go back inside."

"Why?"

Confusion bleeds into my face. "Why not? They're your friends."

"Talon is my friend. Crystal is no one."

A heartbeat passes, and then another, and I'm not sure what to say. Do I tell him about what Crystal said about this morning? Come out and ask him if he's sleeping with both of us? Or is that too straight forward? He told her he wasn't interested, but that doesn't mean he wasn't interested before.

"Did she say something to you?" he interrupts my thoughts with his question. I suppose it's now or never.

Licking my lips, I say, "Not directly. It was more telling the entire cafeteria."

"What did she say?" Jackson crosses his arms over his chest, making himself look more imposing.

I drop my gaze to the floor and stare at my sneakers. "She said that you called her this morning to come over, and that you hung out together last night. I don't really care who you hang out with, but like I told you before, I don't want to catch any diseases or anything, and I don't know who else you're doing stuff with and..." I'm rambling now.

"Shut up," Jackson says sternly, and I feel my heart sink into my stomach. Things were going so well. Why did I have to go and screw them up?

Goosebumps break out across my skin when Jackson's fingers grip onto my chin, forcing me to look up and into his forest green eyes, in the sun, they seem a shade lighter than usual.

"If I wanted to fuck someone else, I would. The only person I'm doing anything with is you, and I literally can't stand Crystal. I don't want her, and we aren't friends."

I nod or at least try with his grasp holding my head in place. My shoulders suddenly feel lighter, and warmth fills me, knowing he isn't with anyone else but me.

"Oh, okay. You didn't... you didn't have to tell me. We aren't anything. You said it yourself, we're not even friends."

A ghost of a smile tugs at Jackson's lips. "We're complicated, to say the least, and I didn't have to say something. But I'm dicking you, so you deserve to know if I'm doing the same to other girls, which I'm not."

"Dicking?" I can't help but giggle at the term. "Is that even a word?"

"It is now," he says, grinning. "Seriously, though, I wouldn't do that to you."

I shouldn't even ask, shouldn't even contemplate saying the word, but my mouth gets the word out before I can stop it. "Why?"

He shrugs. "I wouldn't allow you to sleep with someone else. So, it's only fair I extend the same courtesy to you."

And in a roundabout way, I feel like he respects me more. That he's seeing me for more than what I did and who I took from him.

We both lost Jillian that day, and though we didn't die, whatever we shared did. I want that back more than anything in the world because when I'm with Jackson, everything seems a little brighter, a little easier.

23

JACKSON

A week passes, and things with Kennedy remain the same. I hate admitting how much better I feel when we're together. It still seems like I'm betraying Jillian by befriending Kennedy, and it takes an enormous amount of effort to remind myself daily that that's not the case.

My mind is assaulted by images of Kennedy from the night that we shared dinner together. Her smile, the way she opened up to me. It's not new, we'd always been friends, so I don't know why it's so different, but it feels like we're just becoming friends for the first time.

Walking out of my business class, I wait in the courtyard for Kennedy to show. She should be coming from her economics class soon. Tugging my phone out of my pocket, I settle on a bench and let the warmth of the sun beat down on me.

Going to my messages, I find three brand new ones from my best friend from high school, Ty. He goes to North Woods University, so I haven't seen him in almost a year.

I grin as I scroll through the messages.

Ty: What up, man?

. . .

TY: Dude, really? Ignoring me?

TY: Can't ignore me if I'm there, right?

TY: Psst. I'm here, and the fucking chicks are *flame emoji*

I'M NOT SHOCKED at all that he just showed up here, and I'm actually happy he's here. With a fight at the pits tonight and a party over at the frat house, he's come at the perfect time. Typing out my response, my finger moves over the send key when I feel someone walking up behind me.

"Guess who?" Ty's dumbass voice filters into my ear, and I twist around to face him.

"Hey, dumbass," I say, snickering. "I was just about to text you back."

"Yeah? After I already sent you four messages. I see where I rate." Crossing his arms over his chest, I can see he's been working out more. He was always kind of athletic, and girls flocked to our group of friends all the time. Ty was a lady killer, and I'm sure he still is.

"I was in class, what do you want me to do, pull out my phone, and message you back right away?" Conceited bastard obviously still thinks the world revolves around him.

Ty taps his chin. "Actually, yeah, I do."

Walking around the bench, he takes the spot next to me. "What are you doing sitting out here? People watching? Or pussy watching?"

Do I tell him about Kennedy? Probably not. There isn't anything going on between us, but yet I'm sitting on the bench waiting for her to come out of her class.

I decide to tell him a little white lie, then if Kennedy comes out, I can pretend like I didn't see her or something if she asks. "Just sitting here. It's nice out, and maybe I wanted to catch some rays?"

Ty chuckles, running his fingers through his dark brown hair.

"What are we doing this weekend? Partying? Chicks? I didn't come here just to sit on a park bench."

Twisting around, I pin him with a stare. "Dude, you've been here five minutes, chill."

Ty shrugs, and I look away, hoping he'll chill the fuck out. Maybe he's on something? Wouldn't be the first time, and would explain why he's so hyped up, his knee bouncing up and down and his hands moving, tapping against his thighs.

Students come rushing out of the economics hall, and my heart beats a little bit faster. I feel anxious as I watch, waiting for her blonde head to appear in the crowd. I shouldn't be watching for her, waiting, wanting to spend any more time than I do with her, but I can't help myself. Being around her makes me feel better.

Spotting Kennedy in the crowd, I suppress a smile.

"Holy fuck, is that Kennedy?" Ty leans over, nudging me in the side as if I'm not already looking right at her.

"Yeah, she goes to school here." I try not to show my disgust at him saying her name. I don't want him to even remotely know that I care about her.

"I thought this was a fancy-ass school. How did they let someone like her in? I still can't believe they let her go." Ty shakes his head, and I have to fight the urge to sucker punch him for talking about her like that. Then he does something that I never expected.

"Hey, killer!" he yells as she descends the steps. She looks up, and her face becomes ashen. Her gaze bounces like a ping pong ball from Ty and back to me before she finishes descending the steps and turns around the corner.

"What the fuck?" I growl, turning to Ty.

"What?" He seems legitimately confused. I'm pissed, so fucking angry that he said something like that, and more so that I was sitting next to him while he did it.

"You can't just go around yelling shit like that." I sigh, frustrated with Ty and my feelings for Kennedy.

Ty's gaze widens with shock. "Why not? I mean, you of all people should hate her the most. She got into a car drunk and killed your sister."

"I know!" I almost scream out in frustration. I'm angry with him, with myself, the whole situation. "I fucking know what she did. But I also know that she's been through enough. She lost Jillian too, and it's not like she did it on purpose. Hating her isn't going to bring her back." Ty looks at me like I've grown a second head.

"Well, damn, I didn't know you would actually forgive her for what she did. Especially considering..." He trails off, looking anywhere besides me.

"Considering what?"

"Nah, man, I shouldn't tell you."

"Tell me, what? Out with it, Ty."

"Man, I probably should've told you this earlier, but I didn't want to make things worse, but that night... Kennedy came on to me."

"What?"

"Yeah, man, she begged me to fuck her, and I wouldn't. She left so quickly because I rejected her. She wanted to be with you and thought if she used me to make you jealous, you would finally notice her." Ty releases a laugh. "Funny, seems she got everyone's attention."

For one whole minute, I just sit there. I don't even think I'm breathing. The content feeling fades away, and the darkness, the hate, it all comes flooding back to me. In an instant, my thoughts flip. It's like being struck by lightning.

"Sorry, I didn't tell you sooner," Ty's voice pierces the fog.

I can't even speak, my jaw is clenched so hard, my hands are curled into tight fists, and the blood in my veins is itching for violence. I'm afraid if I get up right now, something bad is going to happen, and yet I can't fucking sit here and wait.

I'm furious, she fucking played me. It wasn't just her getting in the fucking car and driving drunk. She did it for a selfish reason, got in the car and left, unable to wait for me, probably because she didn't want me to know that she tried to get my best friend to fuck her.

My sister died because Kennedy wanted to be a selfish fucking bitch.

Shoving off the bench, I start running in the direction Kennedy went. I'm consumed with a need to make her pay, to rip her heart from her fucking chest.

If she thought she could play me, soften me, with her little pity story about cutting, or use my emotions against me, she thought wrong.

"Jackson, wait up. Where are you going?" Ty yells behind me.

I don't even look back as I continue walking. "To find her!"

24

KENNEDY

He's here. Why is he here? My feet can't seem to move fast enough as I sprint down the sidewalk and through the throngs of people congesting my route of escape.

"Where's Jackson now? Who's going to protect you?" I can hear his voice ringing in my ears, feel his fingers digging into my flesh. Tears prick my eyes at the memory.

I'm drowning, suffocating in fear. Walking a little faster, I dart through the crowd and almost sag to the ground once I'm past everyone. Gripping the straps of my backpack, I start walking again, but I've only taken one step before someone grabs me by my backpack, hauling me backward. A scream lodges in my throat but becomes nothing more than a muffled squeak.

"Did you think you could use me? That you could play me?" Jackson's rage-filled voice burns the tips of my ears. I try to twist around in his grip, but it's no use as I almost trip over my own feet while he drags me behind him. *What is happening?*

Tugging me around a corner, I don't realize that I'm trapped between two buildings until Jackson shoves me against the brick exterior. Like a bear, his body looms over mine, blocking out any slivers of sunlight.

I shiver at the feral look in Jackson's eyes, and that's when I see him. Tylor. *Oh, god.* This can't be happening. Placing a hand against my stomach, I try to combat the need to vomit. I have to get away, have to escape before he hurts me.

"Answer me!" Jackson yells into my face. His fingers dig into my upper arms as he gives me a shake as if he is trying to shake a response out of me. His grip is so tight, my arms hurt. The same hands that caressed me last night, now leave bruises on my skin.

"I..." Is the only thing I can get past the lump in my throat. Only then do his words trickle into my fear-stricken mind. *"Did you think you could use me? That you could play me?"* What is he talking about? I shake my head, trying to tell him that I don't understand, but he only shoves me against the wall again. My head bounces off the brick, and I welcome the pain. It's better than the fear, better than the throbbing ache in my chest.

My vision blurs with tears, but I can still make out Tylor standing right next to us, a sinister smirk on his face.

"You're a selfish bitch, and I can't believe that I fell for your act, that I even considered forgiving you."

I'm so confused.

"What?" I ask, my voice cracking in two at the end.

"Come on, killer, you didn't think I wasn't going to tell him, did you?" Tylor's voice is like acid touching my skin, and when he touches his crotch, bile rises in my throat. I want to scream, to fight, to tell Jackson that whatever he told him isn't true, but I can't get the words out.

Jackson's entire body trembles with indescribable rage, and I flinch, afraid that he may actually hurt me. I've never seen him so angry, seen him so close to the edge.

"I thought if I showed you that I cared, we could both heal, but I realized today that you don't deserve to heal. You deserve to suffocate, to drown in your own pain and misery." Then he leans into me, his lip curled—I turn away, afraid of what may happen if I look him in the eyes—as he whispers, "Cut yourself a little deeper next time."

He doesn't know it, but his words cut me deeper than any wound I could ever inflict on myself. He could throw me to the wall hard enough to crack my skull, and it wouldn't hurt as much as *this*. Deep down, I knew I shouldn't have trusted him. I ate out of his open palm, letting him feed me lies, and make me believe something that was far too good to be true.

Between Jackson's anger and Tylor's presence, I'm in my own personal hell.

With one final shove, he releases me, and I slump back against the wall. I'm broken, a wound pulsing with blood, and soon I'll bleed out. Rearing his arm back, he swings it at me like he's going to punch me. The air swishes past my face, and I close my eyes and wait for the pain, but it never comes.

I feel the impact of his fist against the wall, and when I pry my eyes open, I find him standing in front of me, blood dripping down his clenched fist. He's looking straight at me with nothing but unbridled hate and betrayal in his eyes. Everything we shared these last few days, every happy moment, every kiss, and every touch has been erased from his mind. In an instant, I've become nothing to him.

For every step we took forward, we just took twice as many back.

"I hate you, and I regret ever meeting you. I regret touching you. I regret everything between us," he spits the words at me before turning around and walking away. Tylor stands there for another second, a wide smile spread across his face. I don't even have to ask because I already know that he did this. He told Jackson a lie, and of course, he believed his friend over me. He didn't even consider that Tylor was lying. He is convinced that I did whatever it is Tylor told him about me.

"Catch you later, baby," he says, low enough so Jackson won't hear before he too, turns around and walks away.

Left in the alleyway all alone, I have a hard time staying on my feet. My knees threaten to give out. All the wounds that were healing, have been ripped wide open. I feel so broken, shattered into a million tiny pieces that no glue in the world can put back together.

I thought I could heal, thought I could get better, but now I know that it was all an illusion. There is no redemption for me. I killed my best friend, and now I'm being punished. Forever punished, and I guess that's what I deserve.

Shut it off. My brain screams as the sadness threatens to consume me.

When I can finally make my legs work again, I use that energy to take myself home. I'm so tired, so exhausted by simply trying to live.

I walk through my door, barely remembering the way to my apartment. My mind and my body feel disconnected somehow. I don't want to be here anymore. I don't want to do this. Fight to live, struggle to breathe.

I just want silence, peace...

On autopilot, I walk into my bathroom and strip out of my pants, remembering his words... *"Cut yourself a little deeper next time."*

With shaking hands, I open the medicine cabinet and find the razor blades in their usual spot. Maybe part of me expected this to happen since I never threw them out. I guess my subconscious knew that my healing was only temporary.

I step into the bathtub and sit down. This will be easier to clean up, I think to myself as I look down at my thighs. It's been a long time since I had a healing scab. Not having cut myself in days has left me without any fresh wounds. I take my legs in one last time, knowing that I'll probably never see them like this again.

My heart pounds against my ribcage as I find a smooth spot on my thigh and bring the blade to my skin. With one flick of my wrist, the sharp razor slices through my skin like a hot knife through butter.

I close my eyes and let my head fall back against the edge of the tub. The cut burns, but my mind relaxes, a calm washing over me in an instant. The constriction on my chest eases, and I feel like I can breathe a little better now. Everything vanishes from my mind, leaving nothing but momentary silence behind. I invite the peacefulness in, trying to hold on to it as long as I can, but like everything else in my pathetic life, it slips from my fingers.

Guilt, sadness, and hopelessness return to me all too soon.

He despises me.

He hates me while I can't stop loving him.

Does he know I love him?

He probably wouldn't care either way. His face enters my mind, and I can't shake how he looked at me with so much disgust and hate.

He doesn't love me, and he wouldn't care if I died. No one would care if I wasn't here. Not him, not my parents… no one.

No one would care.

Finding another spot, I make another cut. Slicing so deep, that blood trickles down both sides of my thigh. Another wave of serenity washes over me, drowning my mind into silence. My eyes roll back, and my head lulls to the side. I feel sated, calm, and satisfied, but I know the feeling won't last long. I want it to last forever. Each slice is like another hit, another pulse-pounding euphoria.

With my eyes shut and my head leaning back, I bring the blade back to my skin without looking or thinking, slicing again before the bad thoughts and feelings can return. I don't want to let those demons back in, it's too much to take.

I can't do this anymore.

I continue cutting myself, never even opening my eyes to see what I'm doing. I just keep cutting, banishing everything ugly away and welcoming the peace and quiet I desperately long for. I slice and slice until the blade slips from my fingers, and my hands slide off my leg.

I try to move, try to find the blade, but my fingers won't listen to my commands. My limbs feel impossibly heavy, my mind drowsy like my head is underwater. Trying to open my eyes, I can't. They're weighed down with cinder blocks. Movements are impossible.

My body is useless, just like my existence.

No one wants me.

No one needs me.

Everybody will be better off when I'm gone.

That's the last thing I think of before my mind slips into the darkness with open arms.

25

JACKSON

Walking into the pit, I feel nothing. Not a damn thing. I'm so far from gone when it comes to my emotions, I might as well be in another universe. Blocking out everyone around me, I don't hear the chants or feel the thundering beneath my feet. I bounce on my heels, cracking my neck and stare off into space, waiting for Franco to announce the fighter.

Tylor is standing just outside the pit with Talon. They're whispering to each other, and I'm getting more agitated as the seconds pass.

"Where the fuck is this guy, Franco?" I snarl.

"I don't know," he replies without looking away from his phone. "If he's a no-show, then we're fucking screwed. Bets have already been placed, and everyone is already here. I'll look like a joke if I don't find someone to replace him within the next five minutes." Sheer panic shadows his features.

"You'll also be dead because if I don't have someone to fight, I'm taking out your ass." Franco looks away and starts typing out something on his phone.

Talon and Tylor jump down into the pit. Talon turns to me first. "What's going on?"

"Franco's guy is a no-show, and I have no one to beat the fuck out of. Who the fuck is this guy, not showing up for a ten-grand paycheck?"

I need someone, anyone, because if I don't get this fire out of my veins. If I don't drain the anger from my body, I won't be able to stop myself from going to her. From truly hurting her in the same way she hurt me.

My muscles tighten with tension that needs to be released.

"Ten-grand?" Ty asks, rubbing his chin. "I wouldn't mind that kind of paycheck."

"Depending on what bets are made, even more. Jackson made twenty-five grand the last time he fought," Talon explains.

"I'll fight you, dude," Tylor interjects, shocking the hell out of me.

"You'll fight me?" I almost laugh. "You're joking, right?"

It has to be the money talking.

Tylor's features become serious. "No. I've been working out a lot more, and I know you need someone to fight, so let's do this." Pulling his shirt off, he starts stretching his arms. I glance at Talon, who looks just as surprised as I feel.

"Dude, I'm not going to take it easy on you because you're my friend. Inside the pit, you'll be nothing more than my opponent for the night."

"Are you scared I'll beat your ass in there and embarrass you in front of all your new friends?" Ty asks, confidence dripping from his voice.

Does he really think he stands a chance against me?

If I wasn't so hell-bent on fighting, I might care that I'm about to smash one of my best friends' faces in, but I don't. If he thinks he can take me, then I'll gladly show him otherwise.

"Let Franco know that Tylor is going to step in," I tell Talon.

He nods and walks away to find Franco while I push everything to the back of my mind again. I let Talon wrap my hands and watch him do the same for Ty. Since he doesn't have a mouth guard, I don't put mine in either. Doubt I'll need it anyway.

A few minutes later, Franco's voice fills the warehouse.

"We had a no-show, but no fear, we've found a replacement." The crowd erupts around us, and Tylor shakes his limbs out, looking at me a little too gleefully.

Doesn't he realize that I'm out here to win? This isn't a pissing contest.

We both enter the pit, and I breathe deeply, shutting down all my thoughts, telling myself that the guy in front of me isn't my friend. He is the enemy and nothing more.

Franco talks some more, and there is another loud eruption from the crowd, but I hear nothing. Silence settles in my head. I'm focused, determined, and ready.

"I'll take it easy on you," Ty says, grinning, bouncing around in front of me. Franco rings the fight bell, and the world fades away from me.

I take one small step toward Ty while he takes two large ones toward me, fists raised, ready to fight. His inexperience comes through right away as he takes a wide swing, giving me plenty of time to duck down and jab him in the ribs instead.

He doubles over and stumbles back, looking at me like he didn't expect me to hit him. What did he think this was? High School wrestling?

His cockiness is quickly replaced by his anger. Charging for me, he swings again, a little bit better than the first time, but still nothing I didn't see coming. I easily avoid his fist, twist around and punch him in the side of the head.

This time, I think he is going to fall over. Uneasy on his feet, I give him a minute before hitting him again.

"Dude," he growls, throwing up his hands.

"I told you I wasn't going to give special treatment. You knew what you signed up for when you stepped into this ring."

Blood drips from his busted lip, and he wipes it with the back of his hand. "Wow, that bitch really did a number on you." I know he is bringing her up out of desperation, hoping to throw me off and give himself a chance. What he doesn't realize is that the mention of her only fuels my anger, making me stronger, more vicious.

I move so fast, he doesn't even see the kidney punch coming. I hit him so hard it knocks the wind out of him, and he crumbles to the floor with a groan.

Franco starts to count down, but only gets to three. To everyone's surprise, Ty gets back up. I shake my head at him. He should have just stayed down.

"I don't even know what you like about her," he slurs, ready to pass out. I must have really rattled his brain because his next words make no sense at all. "She can't even suck a dick right. Terrible gag reflex."

"Just tap out, Ty, you're done. You're talking gibberish."

"I know what I'm saying, asshole! I said Kennedy can't suck a dick. I had to hold her down and show her how to do it right that night at the party." He lunges for me, and this time I can't move. His fist connects with my jaw, making my head snap to the side before I can recover, he gets me again in the side of the head, and again in my ribs when I try to turn away.

I know I need to concentrate on the fight, drown everything else out like I always do, but his fucking words are messing with my mind. Did he just say what I think he said? He did what to Kennedy?

His words take hold slowly, almost like I have to digest them one by one. With each of his words reaching my mind, a picture of Kennedy flashes in front of my eyes. Her huddling on the floor when I told her to suck me off. Her choosing sex over a blow job at my place. Her telling me she just can't do it even after I made her come.

The fear in her eyes. The tremble in her voice.

No. Tylor wouldn't have...

I just can't believe my friend would do that.

Ty is raining down punches on me, but I can't feel anything right now. With my fists covering my face, I let him shower me with body shots just so I can think. When I've had enough, I shove him off and drop my arms long enough to look at his face.

And then I see it. The smug grin on his face. The darkness in his eyes.

"You know she turned me down because of you?" He chuckles, and the heavy fog on my mind is lifted. The puzzle pieces lock together, forming a very vivid painting right before my eyes. *He... he hurt her*. My body starts shaking with violence. Every fiber of my being ready to attack, ready to kill. He hurt her...and now I'm going to hurt him.

The next few minutes happen in a blur. One moment I'm looking at Tylor's evil grin, the next, he is passed out, and I'm on top of him. It's like I'm watching myself move outside my body. My fists are coated in blood. I can barely recognize his face when some unknown arms pull me away from his unmoving body. I want him to keep moving, want him to fight back, but all he does is lie there.

When I try to struggle free, I realize that there are three guys with their arms wrapped around me, tugging me backward. I Try to look over them and to the fucker's body. I want to make sure he's unmoving.

"What the fuck was that?" Talon's voice cuts through, even over the crowd cheering me on. "I think you killed him, dude."

Good. I hope I did. Fuck the consequences. I'll gladly live the rest of my life behind bars if he's dead.

Franco rushes to Ty's side and checks his pulse. "He's alive," he announces. "I'll have someone come and check him out. You get him out of here," he tells Talon, but I'm already rushing out.

It feels like an elephant is sat on my chest. I need to get to Kennedy. I need to tell her that I was wrong, that I'm sorry. It all makes sense, everything. Talon yells my name over and over again, but I ignore him, I need to get to her.

Climbing into my SUV, I race out of the parking lot. My hands are slippery as I grip the steering wheel, and I look down to see my hands are covered in blood. I can't seem to be bothered by it, though, because all I can think about is getting to Kennedy and telling her that I fucked up.

My stomach churns, and acid burns up my esophagus at the thought of what he did to her. I want to punch myself in the face, to rip out my heart and put it on a platter, and give it to her. This whole time she's been hurting, and for a multitude of reasons, not just because of Jillian's death but because of the events of that night.

It seems to take forever for me to reach her apartment complex. I barely slam the car into park and turn it off before I'm out and racing inside. I know something is wrong before I even knock. I can feel it deep in my gut. Something is terribly wrong.

I knock once, screaming her name. When she doesn't answer right away, I can't wait another second. This bad feeling snakes through me, and I have to get inside, have to make sure she's okay. Taking one step back, I lift my foot and ram it into the door. The wood easily gives way with the force.

Running into her apartment, I scan the living area quickly before making my way through the rest of the apartment. "Kennedy!"

Silence.

Bursting into the bedroom, I find it empty too, and the bad feeling in my gut expands. I turn to look into the bathroom, and then I see it. A few strands of her silky blonde hair are falling over the edge of the bathtub. The coppery tang of blood tickles my nostrils, it's filling the air and making me sick to my stomach.

Walking into the room, my heart sinks to my feet, then stops beating all together when her entire body comes into view. Blood. There is so much blood. Her legs, her hands, her stomach, it's all covered in blood. I don't even know where it's all coming from.

Dropping to my knees on the side of the tub, I call her name, praying she'll wake up. Her face is pale, and her eyes are closed. My hands tremble as I find my phone. I try and type in the code, but my hands are too bloody, my finger slipping over the screen, but nothing happens. The blood on my hands, making it impossible for me to call for help.

Looking down at Kennedy one more time, I decide I don't care about anything but getting her help. Plucking her up out of the tub, I try not to be bothered by the warmth that covers my hands and belly.

"I've got you. I'm going to take you to the hospital. Don't die on me, Junebug. Do not die on me," I croak, and it feels like I'm losing Jillian all over again. I did this. I pushed her, and I have to save her. I have to be the one to make sure she is okay.

Carrying her out of the apartment, I can hear each drop of blood as it hits the floor. When I reach my SUV, I open the back door and put her in the seat, laying her across them. Then I climb in and drive.

Speeding the entire way there, I don't even think I breathe until I'm outside the ER, climbing out and carrying her inside.

"Dear lord," the nurse says when she spots me. Doctors and nurses rush over and take Kennedy from me, and suddenly everything is moving in slow motion. Sinking to the floor, I place my hand against the cool ground. The tears rush in, and like a dam, I release every ounce of emotion I've been holding back.

Pain. Hate. Anger. Regret. Shame.

I lost Jillian, and now I'm losing her too.

I'm sorry I never told you I loved you...

KENNEDY

Peace... I'm finally at peace. No pain or heartache, no disappointment or guilt. My body is numb, and so is my mind. Darkness surrounds me, wrapping me up in a blanket.

I feel as if my body is floating on a cloud, somewhere in between being awake and asleep. Alive but not quite living. I try to think of where I am and how I got here, but every time I form a thought, it slips away.

For a long time, there is nothing but silence. Only me and my friend, the darkness.

"Yes, she is stable now..." A voice suddenly breaks through to me. It seems far away as if I'm standing in one corner of a large room, and someone is in the other, across from me. Something draws me to that voice. I try to move, but my body and mind don't seem to be connected at the moment.

"No, I won't leave her side, I promise..." The same voice speaks again, a little bit louder now as if he took a few steps toward me. I strain to hear him again, hoping he comes a little bit closer still. His voice is a beacon of light in the dark.

"Okay, I'll see you soon..." He stops talking after that, but the sound of heavy footsteps echo in my ears. I think he's coming closer.

When a large warm hand covers mine a moment later, that thought is confirmed.

Part of me wants to pull away from his touch, while some other part of me craves it. I'm confused by the notion until I hear him say his next words.

"Junebug, please, wake up. Please, be okay... I just need you to be okay."

There is only one person in the world who calls me Junebug... Jackson.

Why is he here? I drag myself out of the heavy fog, fighting with all my might to open my eyes. Cinder blocks weigh them down, but somehow, I blink my lids open. Light blinds me, and I release a groan at the burning of my retinas.

Like paint seeping into paper and spreading in large splotches, the events that got me here unfold in my mind. *The cutting. All the blood.*

I flinch when Jackson squeezes my hand gently, reminding me that he's here now.

Cut yourself a little deeper next time...

My entire body is one big ache, and my head is heavy, swimming with thoughts.

"Thank fuck you're okay!" Jackson says, sighing as if he's been sitting here watching me for hours.

Tugging my hand from his, I scowl at him. "Don't touch me!" The words come out so raspy and distorted, I'm not sure if he even understood them.

Anguish contorts his features.

Why is he here?

"I'm sorry, Kennedy. I'm so fucking sorry. This is all my fault. I'll do whatever it takes to make this better. Whatever you want. Tell me, and I'll do it."

"Leave," I croak, trying to scoot away, but my limbs are still too heavy.

"Anything but that. I won't leave you and not only because I promised your mom. I'm not leaving because I love you."

Love? Is he serious?

All I can do is shake my head at him. How can he be talking about love right now? After what he did to me... what he said? I can't wrap my head around it all. It's too much. Too many emotions and thoughts rushing to the surface all at once.

"Please, go..."

"I can't, bug. I can't leave you. Not after I almost lost you forever."

Closing my eyes, I turn my head away from him. I don't want to see him right now, because every time I look at his face, I see him yelling at me. Telling me to cut myself while Tylor is standing next to him, grabbing his crotch. This is worse than my worst nightmare because it's my reality.

"I won't touch you or even talk to you if that's what you want, but I'll be staying here so I can watch over you." I hear him retreating from me and taking a seat in the corner of the room. The tension eases from my body only slightly.

I try to go back to sleep, but my head hurts, and the skin on my legs burns too much to find any rest. When I attempt to move again to get comfortable in another position, I yelp out in pain as I tug on something connected to my arm.

"Hold on, don't move. Let me get the nurse." Jackson jumps up and rushes to my side. He grabs something behind me, and a moment later, a female voice comes through a speaker.

"Nurses station."

"She's awake and needs some more pain meds."

"I'll be right there." The line goes dead, and Jackson takes a step back.

I can only manage to look at him briefly before I turn my head away from him again. Seeing his face hurts too much right now. It's nothing but a reminder of what he said to me. How he treated me. I trusted him, and he betrayed that fragile trust. He believed Tylor's lie about me without even asking my side of the story. How could he believe what he told him? Does he think so little of me? I thought we were getting somewhere, letting go of the past. My chest aches at the thoughts rushing through my brain.

Thankfully, the nurse comes in, pulling a small cart behind her, sidetracking my thoughts.

"How are you feeling?" she asks, walking up to my side. She doesn't smile, but her demeanor isn't mean, just serious.

"Okay." The lie rolls off my tongue so easily.

"On a scale from one to ten, what's your pain at right now?"

One million. But that's just the ache in my chest over the betrayal.

"Eight," I tell her. "Maybe a nine. My head hurts."

"You lost a lot of blood. And the doctor found a bump on the back of your head, you must have hit it on the bathtub."

Or on a brick wall. I should say it out loud. Tell her that I want Jackson gone, that he is the reason I'm hurting, but some small part of me won't let the words escape.

"I'm going to check your vitals and then give you some more pain meds through your IV." She starts wrapping the blood pressure cuff around my arm and takes my pulse while the machine is working, squeezing my arm tightly almost to the point of pain.

"Blood pressure is good," she tells me after she is done. Then she gets a syringe from her cart and injects something into my IV. It only takes a few seconds before I feel the effects. A warm fuzzy feeling spreads through my veins, covering me like a soft heavy blanket.

Exhaustion takes hold of me once more, and with the pain disappearing, I can finally close my eyes and escape the world again.

~

THE NEXT TIME I wake up, someone is holding my hand. I know instantly it's not Jackson. These hands are smaller, softer, and less warm. Prying my eyes open, I come face to face with my mother.

"Hey, honey," she coos, a sad smile on her lips.

"Hey, Mom. What are you doing here? You didn't have to come all this way. I'm fine."

"Oh, Kennedy, of course, I came. You're my child. Why didn't you call me? Why didn't you tell me..." She doesn't finish the sentence, but

I know what she is thinking. Why didn't you tell me that you were hurting yourself... that you wanted to end your life?

The real question is, what would she have done? I'm pretty sure the answer to that is nothing. She would have brushed it off, told me to get out more, make friends, and be normal.

"I'm sorry." I don't even know what I'm apologizing for, but I feel the need to say the words. "It won't happen again."

"It better not," I hear my father's gruff voice from the other side of the room. Only then do I register the other two people in the room. My father is sitting in a chair in the corner, looking down at a newspaper. He doesn't even look at me.

My gaze swings to Jackson, who is leaning against the wall with his arms crossed in front of his chest, staring daggers at my father.

"Travis, now is not the time," my mother warns, but there is not much conviction behind her statement, which eggs my father on even more.

"When is a good time, Claudia? After she kills herself? After she makes a mockery out of this family yet again?"

Instead of saying anything else, my mom just lowers her head and squeezes my hand.

"Get out," Jackson's voice booms through the room. Both mine and my mom's head snaps up to find Jackson looking furious.

"What?" My father looks up from his paper like he can't believe Jackson is brave enough to say something.

"You heard me, old man. Get the fuck out," Jackson growl.

"How dare you—" My father starts but is cut off by Jackson's hand, grabbing a fist full of his shirt to drag him from his chair.

"*How dare I?* How dare you talk to her like that? You're her father. You're supposed to care for her, not make her feel worse. You're part of the problem, and I'm not standing by and letting her be hurt anymore."

My father struggles, but Jackson is too strong. He easily shoves my father out of the room while my mother and I watch the scene unfold with our mouths hanging wide open. Jackson slams the door shut, and I jerk at the sound.

Without saying another word, Jackson walks back to the corner and sits down on the chair my father was in just moments ago.

"I'm going to check on your father," Mom whispers, and I almost roll my eyes. Of course, she worries more about him than me. I nod, and her hand slips away. She steps outside, leaving me alone with Jackson.

"It's too late, Jackson. Standing up for me now doesn't make up for what you did yesterday."

"I know, but I won't leave you. Even if you don't want me right now. I know you need me. Your parents just proved that."

"What I need is space, from you, from them, from everybody. I just want to be left alone."

"I can't do that. I'll give you all the time in the world, I won't expect anything from you, but I won't leave your side."

If he had said those words to me twenty-four hours ago, I would have been happy, ecstatic even. Now, it just drives the knife deeper. Because right now, everything he does is just a reminder of what he didn't do yesterday... protect me.

27

JACKSON

*E*very time I look at my hands, I see her blood on them. I see her pale face, her closed eyes, and pale pink lips. I almost lost her. Had I not got there when I did, she may not be here right now. Hell, what am I saying? She wouldn't be in this hospital bed if it wasn't for me.

Cut yourself a little deeper next time.

I want to rip my own tongue out for saying something so disgusting, so cruel, so horrendous. I knew she was suffering, but my own fragile state overshadowed that. I was selfish and believed someone else without stopping to ask her what really happened. She was the one hurting the most. Jillian died, and the loss of her crushed me, but Kennedy went through so much more than the loss of her best friend.

Had I been at the party that night and not thinking with my dick, maybe none of this would've happened. Maybe Kennedy wouldn't have been assaulted, maybe Jillian would still be here.

I've been so busy piling the blame on Kennedy that I've never stopped to think about how I played into the situation.

"Are you sure about this?" Kennedy's mother asks for the third time.

I nod. "Yes. I'll stay with her and make sure nothing happens."

The apprehension on her face tells me she doesn't want to believe me, but, truthfully, she doesn't have a choice. Kennedy is old enough to make her own choices. She, however, can't be trusted to stay alone. The doctor recommended someone stay with her for the next few weeks. The other option would be to put her into a mental hospital, which is only happening over my dead body. Her father, of course, was all for it, which almost earned him a fist in his face.

"He said he'll call us if there is a problem, Claudia, let's go," Travis, Kennedy's father says, his eyes refusing to meet mine. He's lucky he's even allowed in the room after all the shit he pulled.

"Okay, okay. I'm just worried. I don't want to lose her," Claudia says, her voice cracking. Kennedy hasn't said but a handful of words to her parents. I haven't dared tell her mother that I might be the worst person for this job, given Kennedy's and my past, but I owe her this. I owe it to her to make things right, to protect her, to make sure she gets another chance at this. I can't let her go, not knowing that I'm the cause.

Claudia pats Kennedy on the leg, but she doesn't even look up and acknowledge her mother. "The doctors are going to get you set up with a therapist. You need to go once a week. Please, don't hurt yourself, please. If I lose you…"

"Let's go, honey," Travis growls from the doorway.

I want to tell the fucker that he should care more about his daughter, but you can't make someone care. They either do, or they don't.

Claudia wipes some tears from her face and kisses Kennedy on the forehead before walking toward the doors, turning toward me before she reaches the threshold. "Please, take care of her, and call me if anything happens, day or night."

"Will do," I tell her. She nods and walks out of the room without looking back. I hate how self-absorbed Kennedy's parents are. They should've seen how much she was hurting.

I should've seen how much she was hurting.

"Are you ready to go?" I ask, keeping my voice gentle.

She doesn't look at me as she speaks, "Why are you still here?"

Patience isn't my strong suit, but I'll do anything for Kennedy, so I bury my emotions and remind myself it's going to take time. She is not going to accept me being here.

"I promised your mom I would stay and take care of you so you can continue going to school. I didn't think you wanted to go home."

"I don't, but I also don't want to be with the person that pushed me into this hospital bed."

Fuck that stings, but I deserve that. I deserve to feel her anger and pain. I'm ready to be battered by her because I fucking deserve it. I'll be her whipping post, and the person she needs to hold her together.

"I understand that, and I'm going to make this right. Fix everything that I did."

"I'm not a broken picture frame. You can't fix me."

"I'm not trying to fix you, bug. I'm fixing myself. I'm here because I want to be. Because I owe it to you."

"I don't want you here." She lifts her gaze, and there's a haunting look in her eyes. I want to go to her, wrap my arms around her and tell her everything is going to be okay, but I wouldn't dare. Not now. It's too soon.

"I know, but I'm here, and that's not going to change." Exhaling, I look down at my hands. *Blood. So much blood.* I'll never be able to forget the way I found her. The fact that I caused her that much pain and pushed her to kill herself. I owe her this. "Are you ready to go?" I ask again.

She doesn't say anything, and I decide to take the initiative to get us going. Maybe she'll feel better when we get back to her apartment. Calling for the nurse, I get her a wheelchair and wheel it into the room.

Kennedy pretends as if I'm not there as she slowly pushes off the bed and into a standing position. Pain flicks across her features, and I feel it in my gut, like a dull knife blade digging into my skin. Out of reflex, I offer her my hand, but she smacks it away, hissing at the contact, almost as if I've burned her.

"Let me help you," I plead.

"No," she grits out through her teeth. "I'd rather feel every ounce of pain than let you touch me again."

Her words pelt me like blocks of ice, but I expect them. Expect her to lash out, to hate me, to curse me forever.

The nurse returns a moment later with discharge papers.

"Please, remember to inspect the wounds and make sure that they're clean. We've sent over an antibiotic and pain reliever to the pharmacy. The doctor would like her to resume classes in a few days. If you have any problems, give us a call."

Kennedy grunts and takes the papers from the nurse, scribbling her name across the signature area.

"Thank you," I tell the nurse and start to wheel her out of the room. We make it to the front doors, and I park the wheelchair before turning to her.

"I'm going to go get my SUV, I'll be right back." As expected, I get no response, and she turns her head away from me like a child. I go and get my car, driving up to the pick-up area as fast as I can. I almost sigh with relief when I find Kennedy still sitting there, her hands in her lap. God, she looks so fragile and broken.

I did that to her. I broke her.

Putting the SUV in park, I get out to help her out of the wheelchair, but she's already pushing out of it and hobbling toward me.

"I'm here to help you," I growl, unable to hide my anger. She's going to end up ripping her stitches if she doesn't let me help her.

"I think you've done enough *helping*," she sneers, forcing me to step out of the way as she reaches the door of the SUV. I'm planning to help her into the vehicle when she hops up all by herself, wincing only once her ass hits the leather.

"If you don't want to have to go home and live with your parents, then you'll listen to me. I'm not going to do anything to hurt you."

Kennedy laughs, but it's not humorous—if anything, it's sad. "I don't trust you, Jackson. I should have never trusted you. Thinking you would be there that night, thinking that you would help me, thinking that you would believe me. I trusted in you and look how that turned out." She looks over at me, and I see nothing of the girl I had loved for years. "I hate you. I hate everything that you represent, and every time I see your face, I'm reminded of how you took his side. I'm reminded of what a horrible fucking person you are, and how I never want to look at your face again because that's all you'll ever be."

Tears fill her eyes, and for one brief moment, I can't breathe, think, or even react. I knew she was angry and sad, going through the motions, but I never... I never thought she could truly hate me. Now, I'm not so sure.

I shove my feelings down, stomping them into the earth as soon as they start to pop up. This isn't about me. This is about her.

"I get it," I say and close the door once she's tucked inside.

The drive to her place–after stopping at the pharmacy–is painstakingly slow. When we pull up to her apartment complex, I'm more than thankful to get out of the car. That relief is short-lived when Kennedy gets out and starts wincing. We have an entire flight of stairs to walk up, and there isn't any way I'm letting her walk them. Knowing this, I let her get to the complex door before I scoop her up gently and cradle her to my chest.

"Put me down," she yells as she tries to push away from me.

"Calm down. I'm just carrying you to the apartment. I don't want you to rip any stitches or anything."

"What do you care? You didn't care about me before. What makes this time any different?" Like a feral cat, she lashes out, her nails sinking into my flesh, but I ignore the small twinges of pain that she evokes over my tense muscles. I'm still not healed from the fight, but my pain is insignificant to the pain that she's endured.

"Down you go," I say and set her down when we reach the door to her apartment. She unlocks it with trembling fingers and shoves the door open, before turning to face me.

"You can sleep in the hall."

"That wasn't the deal, Kennedy, and you know it. I'm sleeping in the apartment on your couch, or we can go to my place and stay there. Whichever works best for you. I'm here for you, that's it."

"I hate that I ever cared about you. That I ever became your friend, and that I ever considered loving you. Leave me alone, or I'll tell everyone that you pushed me to kill myself."

With tears in her eyes, she twists on her heels and walks into her bedroom, slamming the door shut behind her. I carry her things into the kitchen before walking out into the living room. Sagging down onto the couch, my head falls in my hands.

Did I make the right choice coming here? By telling Claudia, I'd watch her?

In an instant, I'm reminded that I did, and all the doubt fades away. I need to help her find her way back to the light. I owe her that, and if she still hates me at the end of this, I'll walk away. If that's what she really wants, then I'll do it. I'll let her go because that's how much I love her. I'll suffer the pain of losing her if it's the best thing for her.

28

KENNEDY

Four days pass in a blur. I only allow Jackson in the bedroom to check my cuts and to administer my pain pills. It takes an enormous amount of effort to shut down my feelings when he's near. His scent surrounds me, lodging itself deep inside of my mind. I want to shove him out the front door, but the truth is I need him. In a second flat, I'll be shoved back into the box my parents want me to live in if I don't allow him to stay here and *babysit* me.

That doesn't mean it's easy though. He's a reminder of everything I want to forget. My mom thought I was trying to kill myself, and that's why I cut myself, but that wasn't true. I don't want to die. I just want the pain to lessen.

I woke up feeling well enough to go back to classes today, so that's what I'm going to do. I'm not sure what Jackson has planned, but I'm going even if he doesn't want me to. Tugging my shoes on, I let out a small sigh at the thought of fighting with him. As soon as I stand up, I feel a slight burn on my thighs and wince at the pain that lances the tender flesh.

There's a knock on the bedroom door, and I ignore it, grabbing my backpack off the floor instead. When I get to the door, the knocking has grown more insistent, and I twist the knob, pulling it open much harder than necessary.

I can feel Jackson's eyes roaming my body, each green orb, a heat-seeking missile against my skin.

"Where are you going?"

"Classes. I'm feeling better, and I don't want to elongate going back. Plus, I've missed enough." I only lift my gaze to the middle of his broad chest. I don't want to see his eyes or face. He's just a reminder of everything I'm begging to forget.

"Are you sure about this, Kennedy? I'm not sure your mental or physical state is ready." I roll my eyes, wishing he would go back to not caring if I was breathing or dead.

"I don't really care what you think. I'm leaving, and you don't have to follow me. In fact, I would be grateful if you didn't." Shoving past him, an electrical current rips through me as my arm brushes against his. This would all be so much easier if I didn't feel drawn to him. If my heartbeat didn't spike in his presence.

"No can do, Kennedy. Let me grab my stuff, and then we can leave," he says, and I'm thankful he isn't fighting me on this. I don't really have the strength to argue with him right now anyway. Going into the kitchen, I grab an apple and make a quick cup of coffee, putting it in my travel mug.

When I'm done, Jackson is waiting at the door, and this time, I don't stop myself from looking at him. Arrogantly beautiful, menacing, and capable of death. He'll make you believe anything and then rip the carpet right out from under your feet.

Walking ahead of him, I make sure my pace is faster than his, which is a pain in the ass since he's taller than me. I manage, though, because I don't want anyone to think we're walking together. When I reach my first class, I almost sigh. The tension in my body makes my muscles ache, and I can't wait to put some space between us.

"Whoa, wait," Jackson calls, his hand landing on my shoulder, stopping me from continuing forward. "I'm going to be here when you get out."

"Can't you just go away," I growl, shrugging off his hold. Every time he touches me, warmth envelops my body. My heart clings to him while my brain knows better, knows the damage he can cause.

I make the mistake of looking up and into his mossy green eyes. "No, I can't just go away, and I won't. I'm going to be up your ass, and I'm going to make sure that you're okay because I owe it to you."

Shaking my head, I take a step back, both wanting and needing to put some distance between us. "You don't owe me a thing, and even if you did, I don't trust you. I don't want anything from you because everything comes at a cost, Jackson, and I'm done paying your prices. I'm done." Turning, I walk away and straight through the double doors. I don't stop until I reach my class and slump down into a seat.

Students filter in, taking their seats, and the professor takes the podium at the front of the room. I do my best to focus on what the professor is saying, jotting down notes, and trying to retain all the information I missed while I was gone. Somehow, it feels like people are staring at me, watching me more than usual, so I end up spending most of the class looking over my shoulder like a crazed person.

A few girls are whispering and looking my way, but I don't catch anyone else watching me. Brushing it off to paranoia, I finish class, and when we're dismissed, I walk down the hall and head to my next class even though I want to run back to my apartment.

Stepping outside, I spot Jackson leaning against a tree, his posture is relaxed, casual, and as soon as he spots me, he pushes off the tree and walks over to greet me.

He wasn't lying, he really was waiting. Which disgusts me and makes me feel warm all at once. I hate that he didn't listen to me, didn't go away when I told him to.

"How was class?" he asks.

"Fine. You know you don't need to follow me around, your friends are going to start asking questions if you do."

Jackson shrugs. "I don't really care what they ask or what they say. All I care about is you and what you think and feel."

My mouth pops open, and I'm not really sure what I plan to say, but I guess it doesn't matter because Crystal comes walking up to us, her shoulder slamming into mine, causing me to almost crash into Jackson.

"Oh, sorry, I didn't see you there," She says, chuckling beside Jackson. "Wait, I thought you..." She makes a motion of cutting her wrists and then says, "Looks like you didn't do a good enough job if I do say so myself."

I'm not really shocked at her words, of course, someone as selfish and heartless as her would say something like that. It's fitting, really.

Jackson reacts before I can, grabbing her by the arm and twisting her around to face him. "What the fuck? You think it makes you look cool to say shit like that?" The anger that contorts his face is scary as hell, but a look that I've seen a few times myself.

Still, it's strange to see him directing that rage at someone else, especially a girl that I know would do anything to be with him.

"Let go of me, you're hurting me," Crystal whimpers, tugging her arm from his grasp.

"I'll do more than hurt you if you talk to her like that again," he seethes, and Crystal takes a step back, her nose in the air.

"I can't believe I ever thought of hooking up with you." The disgust on Crystal's face makes her look as if she's tasted something sour.

Jackson laughs. "Like you had a chance in hell. Run along, and if you talk any more shit about Kennedy, you'll be answering to me."

Crystal turns on her high heels and walks away. Though it was very entertaining to see Jackson stick up for me, it changes nothing. It can't. I can't be with someone who hurt me like he did, who used my weakness against me. He knew how broken I was, knew how much I was hurting, and he still hit below the belt.

"You okay?" Jackson's question slices through my thoughts.

"I'm fine." I hold my head high, ignoring the stares we've earned from the little spat.

Wrinkles of worry form against Jackson's forehead. "I'm sorry she is such a bitch."

I shake my head. "Don't apologize. I'm used to being beat down and treated like shit. I'll survive, plus, it's not like it's the first time someone told me to kill myself." I smile, knowing it's a low blow, but I don't care. He hurt me, ripped my heart out of my chest. He deserves to feel my pain, and it doesn't matter how I deliver said pain.

"I deserve that..." He nods as if he's reading my mind.

"I've got to go to my next class," I say, pushing past him.

"Of course, let's go." He turns to follow me. It's annoying, and I grit my teeth to keep the words inside my mouth.

∽

TWO CLASSES LATER, and Jackson is still waiting for me after each class. I figured he would get bored after the first class, but he's still following me around like a lost puppy. Anger grows, pulsing deep in my chest.

"I don't want your pity, and I want you to stop following ome," I growl, walking right up to him. He looks down at me with an impassive look on his face. His green eyes twinkle in the afternoon sun. Why does something so cruel, so dangerous, get to be so gorgeous?

"I don't pity you, and I'm not following you. I made a promise, and I'm sticking to it. I've screwed up a lot over the last couple of months. I didn't ask questions, didn't think things through, and that's my fault. I don't want to lose you, though, and I'm going to do everything I can to make sure I don't."

"You'll be trying for a while then." I cross my arms over my chest, irritated and ready to go home.

"Do your worst to me, Kennedy, god knows, I deserve it. Push me away, hate me, fight me, draw my blood, and rip my damn heart out, but I'm not going anywhere. I will be here every day, as a rock you can lean on or a damn post you can whip your anger at."

I don't tell him what he says makes me smile.

I don't tell him anything. I don't react at all.

I just walk away, heading toward my apartment and allow him to think whatever he wants to think. I won't let Jackson know a damn thing, because I'm not interested in heartbreak warfare. I'm interested in living because I'm done simply surviving.

29

JACKSON

My back is one giant ache. It's so stiff I can barely move around. I feel like an old man needing a cane to walk, grunting every time I stand up straight. Sleeping on Kennedy's couch is killing me, but I'd rather take this pain ten times over than leave her.

Kennedy hasn't talked to me much, she tries to ignore me most of the time, but at least she doesn't tell me to leave anymore. She gave up on that a few days ago when she finally realized I'm not going anywhere.

The only time we've been separated is when one of us is in class. I skipped all my classes for a week, so I could take and pick her up from each of hers, but I knew I couldn't do that forever. I'm planning to start going back this week. I just wanted to give Kennedy a chance to get back into the swing of things.

Twisting and turning on the couch, I try to get comfortable even though I know there is no way. Defeated, I roll off onto the ground and stretch out. It's not as soft as the couch, but at least I can lie flat and don't have to tuck my legs in.

Closing my eyes, I wonder if Kennedy would let me buy her a new, more comfortable couch. Or maybe I could get her to move into my apartment, where we'd have more space. *Yeah right.*

I'm about to fall asleep when my phone buzzes on the coffee table.

I grab it and see Talon's name flashing on the screen. What does he want now? I push the green answer button and hold the phone to my ear.

"What's up?"

"Hey, loser. You're not in bed, are you? You sound like you're half asleep."

"I'm trying to go to sleep, but some asshole called me."

"Dude, it's not even ten."

"Kennedy goes to bed early, and I don't want to keep her up while I watch TV," I explain, not caring about how much I sound like a pussy.

"Okay, Grandpa. I'm really only calling to tell you that your *friend* is still at the hospital. He's awake, but he hasn't said anything. Told the cops, he was mugged by two guys in an alley. Didn't see their faces, of course. I don't think you have to worry about him."

"I wasn't worried about him. He should be worried about me since when he gets out of the hospital, I'll be planning on putting him right back in it. Or maybe I'll kill him this time. He deserves it for what he did to Kennedy."

"I know, man... I know." I told Talon what Tylor did when Kennedy was in the hospital. I had to tell someone, and I needed Talon to understand. "I'll keep you updated on the situation. If anything changes, you'll be the first one to know."

"Thanks, man."

"Night, night, Grandpa," Talon says, chuckling before the line goes dead.

I place my phone back on the table and hear movement at the bedroom door. Craning my neck, I look up and see Kennedy standing there, leaning against the door jamb like she's been standing there for a while.

"What did you do to Tylor?" she asks, confirming my suspicions of her standing there for a bit.

"What I should have done a long time ago. He fought me in the pit. When he was losing, he thought telling me what he did to you would throw me off. Distract me enough to give him a chance to win. Instead, it did the opposite, and I almost beat him to death. He's still in the hospital *recovering*."

Her hazel eyes go wide, and she stands up a little straighter. "You did what? Why? What if he tells the police?"

Feeling smug, I almost laugh. It's like she actually cares about me.

"Don't worry, bug. He won't say shit. He already talked to the police. Told them he got mugged. Case closed."

"Why would you do something like that?"

"He hurt you. That's reason enough. I would gladly kill him. Matter of fact, I would go to the hospital right now and end his life if you asked me to. If his death would help you get rid of your demons, then I would make it happen." I would do all of it, consequences be damned. If I had to spend the rest of my life in prison just so he wouldn't take another breath, I would.

I mean every single word I say, and Kennedy knows it too. I can see it in her eyes, she believes me. Even if she doesn't want to believe that I'm changing, that I'm not going anywhere, that I'm in this for the long haul, she sees it.

"Why are you on the floor?" she asks, changing the subject.

"Your couch is comfortable to sit on, but there isn't enough room for me to lie flat, so I moved to the carpet. It's fine though, don't worry about me." I almost slap myself in the face after I say it. My back is killing me.

"Oh, okay." She turns around and starts walking back into her bedroom. She only takes one step before twisting back around. "If you swear not to touch me, I'll let you sleep in my bed with me."

I have to bite the inside of my cheek, so I don't grin like a fool. "Okay. I swear. No touching, only sleeping."

"I'm serious, Jackson, touch me, and I'll murder you in your sleep."

Her threat makes me smile, and I climb up off the floor. Grabbing my blanket and pillow, I follow her into her room. I watch her climb into the bed and curl up on one side. I get in on the other, making sure there is a good amount of space between us while I get comfortable, stretching my aching limbs. My back is already thanking me for accepting her offer.

She turns off the light, drowning the room into darkness.

"Good night, Kennedy," I whisper, pulling the blanket up to my shoulders.

"Good night," she whispers back.

It takes me some time to fall asleep, but when I do, it's with her floral scent deep in my nose and the warmth of her body close to mine.

30

KENNEDY

*E*verything seems to fall back into place, the only difference is I have a six-foot-two-inch guy that sleeps beside me every night. Jackson has taken up permanent residency as my roommate. I stopped telling him to leave me alone, mainly because it was a waste of my time and annoying since he didn't listen anyway.

I find my way back into a routine. School, homework, eat, sleep... there is only one thing that's been missing. Since that night, I haven't cut myself. It was part of my life for so long. Part of my day, really. Even with me going to therapy, I struggle every day. It was more than a bad habit—it was an addiction. One that I can't just turn off.

I promised myself and my family that I wouldn't cut myself again, and I haven't... but I have been picking at the scabs. It still gives me some of the pain, some of the release I crave. Problem is, now the scabs are healed.

Standing naked in front of the bathroom mirror, I probe at the pink skin where the largest cut was. I press my finger down as hard as I can, but the release never comes. I stand inside the bathroom for a long time, fighting with myself on what to do. I took the razor blades out of the medicine cabinet, but I hid a few under the sink. Maybe I can just make a tiny cut—

"Kennedy," Jackson's voice comes through the closed door, startling me. I jerk away from the door, my boobs bouncing as I do. "You okay in there?"

"Y-Yes... ah, I'll be right out."

"Are you sure you're okay? You've been in there forever." His tone holds an accusation, and I know what he thinks. What's really fucked up is that I'm mad at him for thinking that I'm in here cutting myself, even though that's exactly what I was thinking about.

Having the urge to prove to him that I wasn't, I unlock the door and pull it open without thinking.

"See, I'm fine," I snap.

His mouth pops open, but no words come out. His eyes go wide as his heated gaze roams my naked body.

"I want sex," I blurt out, and his gaze snaps back up to mine. I know without a doubt, he wants it too. If the lust in his eyes didn't give him away, the growing bulge in his pants would.

"Are you sure?" he says, licking his lips like he just ordered a porterhouse steak.

"Yes. I want you to fuck me. Like you did the first time."

His face falls. "You want me to hurt you?" It's more of a statement than a question, and I hate that he can read me so well.

I shrug. "Maybe just a little."

Instead of answering, he grabs my waist, lifts me up, and throws me over his shoulder like a freaking caveman. "What the hell are you doing?"

He just chuckles and carries me to the bedroom, where he deposits me onto my mattress. I watch as he starts taking off his own clothes, enjoying every second of the little show he is giving me. My mouth goes dry while moisture builds between my thighs. I almost forgot what kind of effect Jackson has on me.

"Spread your legs for me," he orders, his voice deep and raspy.

I do as he says and spread out for him, showing him how much I want this right now, how much I want him. I'm completely exposed. Vulnerable, not only physically but mentally too. I don't want to admit it to myself or him, but I've been depending on him. Every day, I lean on him a little more, even if I don't mean to. I don't understand it at all.

I've been trying to push him away when, in reality, I would be worse off without him.

Crawling onto the bed, his naked body hovers above mine. He's so close, I could reach out and touch him, and so I do. Lifting my hands, I run my fingertips over his hard chest and the chiseled abs. His jaw pops, and he hisses through his teeth.

He's enjoying this more than he's letting on.

"I'll never miss an opportunity to be inside of you, but I won't hurt you. Not now or ever again. I know you're struggling. I know you want to cut and hurt yourself again, but I won't let that happen. I will make you feel good in a different way... make you forget. Okay?"

I nod my head before the last word even leaves his mouth. I want that so badly... I want him so badly. All I need is one second, one single second of silence, and I can continue going. Lowering himself, he blankets my body with his. I can't help but moan when his hard erection presses against my center.

"I'll never get used to how responsive you are to me, soaked and begging for my cock." He buries his face in the crook of my neck and sucks on the skin, eliciting a moan from deep within my chest out of me.

Balancing himself on one arm, he snakes a hand between my legs, his fingertips graze my folds, and I mewl like a cat in heat. It's almost embarrassing how badly I want him right now.

Panting against the shell of my ear, he growls, "So wet, you're like a waterfall, gushing your sweet arousal all over my fingers."

"I need you," I murmur, grabbing onto his biceps, sinking my nails into them.

"Fuck, bug." The arousal, in his words, zings through me. Giving in to my need, he lines himself up at my entrance and slowly pushes in. Lifting my hips, I try to get him to move faster, deeper, but he just shifts with me and continues moving at an agonizingly slow pace.

"Please, Jackson," I whimper, hoping to win him over.

"I'm going to make this last because I don't know when you'll let me do this again," he murmurs against my skin while sliding inside of me to the hilt.

I wrap my arms and legs around him, pulling him even closer until there is no space between us. Until his breaths and heartbeat become mine. Until we're one, encapsulated in time.

Every stroke fills me, heals me, and as the pleasure overtakes the pain, I feel my mind and body forgetting, letting go.

"I want to be inside you forever," Jackson whispers against my lips.

"Yes, don't stop." I lift my hips and press my heels into his ass, urging him to go faster, but he doesn't rush, doesn't move any faster. He takes me slow and steady, bringing me to the edge of pleasure over and over again, making it impossible for me to feel anything but him.

After I've come two times, and we're covered in sweat, Jackson ups his pace a little and explodes deep inside of me. The warmth of his seed inside me gives me a strange comfort. Rolling off of me, Jackson drops to the mattress beside me.

Breathing heavily, we both lie on our backs, staring up at the ceiling. I feel drained but in a good way. I'm content, happy, sated... but I know I won't feel this way for long.

As the fog of lust is lifted, and my endorphin-filled brain slowly returns to normal, the familiar feeling of dread returns. The urge to go into the bathroom and find a blade is on my mind yet again. It's the one thing I can rely on. When it all becomes too much, one cut shuts it off. I don't want to die, that's not what this is about. I need something to help me cope.

I can't rely on my parents, I don't have any friends, and I don't know if I'll ever be able to trust Jackson again. He might be here now, but how long will that last? How long before he changes his mind, how long before he realizes I'm too broken to be fixed?

Tears run down my face without my permission. I try to hide that I'm crying, holding in a sob, my chest cracking, the pain radiating outward, but of course, Jackson looks over to me.

"Are you crying?" He shifts onto his side and pulls me toward him, so we're facing each other. "What's wrong, bug? Tell me."

"I love you," I cry out. "But I can't do this. I can't trust you, not after everything that happened between us. I can't let myself love you and depend on you, knowing that you could leave any day. I need more, something that I don't think you can give me."

"I love you too, Kennedy, and I'm not going anywhere. I know I fucked up. Trust me, I know, but I'm not leaving." He cradles my face with his big hands and uses his thumbs to wipe away some of the tears. He knows I'm fragile, and I've already trusted him once. I can't let myself down again. I can't forget the power that he holds, how with the snap of his fingers, he could be gone again.

"I can't forget what you said that day," I confess. "I can't forget you standing next to Tylor and saying those things to me. I can't forget how you looked at me..."

Without another word, he pulls me into his arms and holds me tight against his chest. "I'm so sorry. You will never know how sorry I am. I know I can't erase what I said and what I did to you, but I will never leave you again. I will prove it to you. I don't care how long it takes for you to forgive me. I don't even care if you never fully forgive me. I would deserve it. But I will not let you down again."

Sucking in a deep breath, I let his scent surround me, let him engulf me and care for me.

I give him part of my heart, hoping he will handle it with care this time. Because I don't know if I can survive another heartbreak.

EPILOGUE

One Year Later

"Isn't it weird being with two guys?" I ask Stella as we sit down with our trays.

"I mean, at first it was a little difficult. Easton and Cam are intense even on their best days. I knew I was meant to be with both of them, but finding an ease into how, and which ways, was tough. We've managed though." Stella beams over her shoulder at Easton.

Just as I pop a grape into my mouth, Jackson swoops in, taking the seat on the other side of me. He places his hand on my thigh, and I welcome his touch, the warmth it brings, the pleasure. Twisting to face him, I smile at him, leaning in to kiss his full lips.

I almost choke on my grape, but it pops back into my mouth a second before I start to panic.

"I guess you know all about rough starts. I'm glad you two were able to figure things out."

"We're complicated," Jackson tells her, grabbing a piece of food off my tray while his green eyes find mine.

"Yeah, love is complicated," Stella says with a smirk. "You belong together just like I belong with Easton and Cam."

Agreeing with her, I nod. I'm so glad that I've found happiness. Jackson didn't lie to me when he said no matter what he was staying. His dedication made it painfully obvious that getting rid of him wasn't going to be easy.

I couldn't forgive him so easily, not until I was ready, and one year later, I think I'm finally there. We've lived together for a year, sleeping in the same bed, having sex, and healing each other, but we never put a label on anything.

"I want to meet up and do a double date or something. With half days for classes, I'm so bored," Stella groans.

"Well, not everyone is a genius like you and gets to take half days for classes," I tease. My friendship with Stella is one of my favorite things. Having a near-death experience lets you think about things differently. So, when she approached me to see how I was after my cutting incident, I took her up on her offer of coffee. We've been friends ever since.

"See, babe, we aren't the only ones who think you're beyond smart," Easton says, tugging her into his side. I can see how much he loves her, how he would go to the ends of the earth to protect her, and back again. It's a lot like how Jackson looks at me.

"Shut up and stop trying to get into my panties," she says, laughing, and Easton's gaze turns possessive.

"We both know I wouldn't have to try, baby." The drop in his voice even makes me shiver. Jackson notices and grips my thigh a little tighter, drawing my attention back to him.

"All right, let's go... I'll talk to you soon. We all definitely need to hang out more," Stella says as she gets up from the table. Easton follows behind her like a puppy, giving me a wink.

Not sure what that was about.

"Hey, you okay?" Jackson pulls me into his side, and I nuzzle my face into the crook of his neck. He still smells like citrus and lemongrass.

"Yeah, I actually wanted to talk to you about something."

"What is it?" The concern in his voice proves to me that it's time. Jackson has spent the last year busting his ass to prove to me that he loves me and that he wants me and only me, and it's time for me to show him that I accept his apology.

"Kennedy, babe, are you still with me?" Jackson asks.

I blink and shake my head, forcing myself to pay attention to the present. Turning to face him, I grab him by the cheeks and pull him to my face. "I want to go somewhere."

"Anywhere you want, I'll go."

"I have to tell you something."

"If you're asking me to leave, it's not—"

"Shh, it's not that. I'm not going to tell you to leave ever again."

One second passes, and then another, and then he's getting up and grabbing my tray from the table. "Let's go."

"I haven't even finished lunch," I squeak.

"I'll get you something in the drive-through on the way to wherever we're going."

"Okay, let's go," I say, jumping up from my seat.

∽

WE STOP at McDonald's on the way out of town since I'm the one doing the driving. I'm sure Jackson knows where we're going, but he doesn't say anything. Instead, we argue over the radio stations and talk about school. It takes us an hour and a half on the interstate to get to North Woods, and when we pull into the cemetery, neither of us says anything. Jackson gets out first and comes over to the driver's side of the car, opening the door and offering me a hand.

A sudden nervousness washes over me. For a long time, I blamed myself. I hated myself because hating myself was easier than admitting that she was gone. It was easier than believing something bad had happened to me, and like a domino effect, everything came crashing down. I miss Jillian every day, and I am thankful beyond measure that Jackson decided to stay and be my rock over the last year.

"We didn't have to come here," he says as we join hands, and I close the car door. The sun is still perched in the sky, and a soft breeze blows through the trees. Everything about this moment feels right.

"We did," I say, turning to him.

Hand in hand, we walk to Jillian's grave. I never got to go to the funeral since I was still in the hospital the day they had it, but I came here on my own to say my goodbyes once I was released. It's the first time Jackson and I have ever been here together, though, and it's special to me because it's like our healing is coming full circle.

Stopping in front of her grave, I stare at the words etched into the stone.

Loving daughter, sister, and friend.

My eyes well with tears as I drag my fingers over the letters.

Turning to face Jackson, I can see the emotions on his face, each flickering with a different degree.

"After everything that happened, I never expected to want to be with you. I was determined to forget that you existed and to move on with my life, but you didn't let me go. You stayed with me through the good and the bad and showed me that you really do care."

"I love you, Kennedy, and I've been telling you that since the day you came home from the hospital. I loved you even when I was hurting you because I was hurting."

I nod, a lump forming in my throat. "I love you too. This last year has made me appreciate you so much, and I wanted to come here to Jillian's grave and tell you that I forgive you. That I love you, and I'm ready to embark on whatever journey is planned for us. I'm ready to be a couple."

Jackson releases my hand and cups me by my cheeks, leaning in to press a gentle kiss to my lips. All I can feel is him, the warmth of his lips, the kindness of his touch.

"I already thought we were," he says, grinning, which in turn makes me smile.

"Technically, we kinda were, but we never made it official, and you never pushed or asked me if I forgave you. You let me heal all on my own, picking me up when I fell down."

Neither of us says anything, we just stand there holding each other, letting the breeze rush past us and into the trees.

"Do you think Jillian would be happy if she saw us now?"

Jackson pulls away but only slightly. "I think Jillian sent us to each other, so we could heal together because she knew even though it was going to be rough that we needed each other."

I nod because I did need him. I needed him so that I could let go of the pain. I needed his anger so I could realize that I wasn't the only one to blame.

"I love you," he whispers.

"I love you too, and I'm glad you didn't leave when I told you to."

"I'm a little bit stubborn." He lets out a chuckle.

"A little bit?" I shake my head and look back at Jillian's grave one last time before we leave to head back to the car.

I miss you, and I'll never stop missing you.

Thank you for giving me your brother.

The End

ALSO BY THE AUTHORS

CONTEMPORAY ROMANCE

North Woods University
The Bet
The Dare
The Secret
The Vow
The Promise
The Jock

Bayshore Rivals
When Rivals Fall
When Rivals Lose
When Rivals Love

Breaking the Rules
Kissing & Telling
Babies & Promises
Roommates & Thieves

***

Also by the Authors

DARK ROMANCE

The Blackthorn Elite
Hating You
Breaking You
Hurting You
Regretting You

The Obsession Duet
Cruel Obsession
Deadly Obsession

The Rossi Crime Family
Convict Me
Protect Me
Keep Me
Guard Me
Tame Me
Remember Me

***

EROTIC STANDALONES

Their Captive

Runaway Bride

His Gift

ABOUT THE AUTHORS

J.L. Beck and C. Hallman are an international bestselling author duo who write contemporary and dark romance.

Find all of our books, links, and signs on our website
www.bleedingheartromance.com

Beck AND Hallman
BLEEDING HEART ROMANCE

- **f** CASSANDRAHALLMAN
  AUTHORJLBECK

- **◉** CASSANDRA_HALLMAN
  AUTHORJLBECK

- **BB** CASSANDRAHALLMAN
  JLBECK

AUDIO BOOKS

All of our book are now either available or on preorder through Audible.

Some of our favorite are...

The Bet, narrated by Teddy Hamilton and Ava Lucas

∽

Kissing and Telling, narrated by Jeremy York and Veronica Landon.

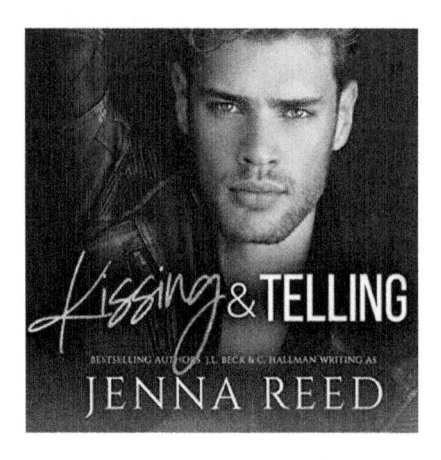

Hating You, narrated by Blake Richards and Olivia Amaro.

When Rivals Fall, narrated by Meghan Kelly.

WARNING
EXPLICIT CONTENT
B
when
rivals
fall
USA Today Bestselling Author
J.L. BECK
ONLY FROM
audible

Printed in Great Britain
by Amazon